James Sutherland

"Ticklesome Tales" Copyright 2017 James Sutherland

Cover Illustration by James Sutherland Copyright 2017

"Norbert" Copyright 2011 James Sutherland

"Roger the Frog" Copyright 2012 James Sutherland

"Ernie" Copyright 2017 James Sutherland

All Illustrations Copyright James Sutherland 2017

Contents:

Norbert

Chapter 1

Norbert stood sheltering from the rain underneath the old sycamore tree that stood in the middle of Finbar's field. It had stopped raining two days ago but Norbert, who was never the most intelligent of horses, had failed to notice. He gazed thoughtfully at the ground beneath his hooves and saw that he had eaten every last blade of grass in that particular patch. For a moment he was baffled, but then something very unusual occurred; Norbert had a thought! *Colin the cuckoo would know what to do...* Snuggled in his nest, high up in the old sycamore tree, Colin was a wise old bird who had known Norbert ever since he was a young foal.

"Are you there Colin?" Norbert whinnied, peering up into the leafy branches above his head.

"Of *course* I'm here!" Colin warbled from high up in his nest, a bit annoyed at being disturbed from his newspaper. "You know I'm too old to get out much these days."

"I'm sorry," said Norbert. "It's just that I've eaten all of the grass under the tree, and I'm still a bit peckish and..."

"Then move out from underneath the tree and eat some of the grass from the rest of the field, you clod-hopping clot!" interrupted Colin. "And *don't* come pestering me with any more of your silly questions!"

Norbert waddled sadly out into the May sunshine. *Why hadn't he thought of that?* Fortunately, he was such a forgetful horse that the unpleasant episode with Colin soon vanished from his mind as he tucked into to the fresh green grass at the other end of the field.

After an hour of chomping and chewing to his heart's content, Norbert realized that he was very thirsty. He had learned over the course of his twenty-seven years in the field that whenever he was thirsty, he needed to pay a visit to the water trough, and so off he went. It was as he leaned over the stone trough to begin his drink that he saw something that made him rear up in terror. *There was another horse peering out of the water at him!* His first instinct was to trot as fast as his tired old legs would carry him back to the old sycamore tree to tell Colin what had happened, but a hazy memory in the back of his mind made him pause. *The last time he had told Colin about the strange horse in the water trough, his feathery friend had been very annoyed.* Norbert tried and tried as hard as he could to remember why…

Eventually after several minutes of intense pondering, he recalled that Colin had explained that he needn't be afraid of the horse in the water trough because it was just his own reflection.

Aha! Norbert grinned a toothy grin. *Wait until I tell Colin how clever I've been!*

First things first, though – he had better have a drink. And so, licking his big rubbery lips with anticipation, he turned back towards the trough, only to rear up in terror once again… *The strange horse was still there, peering up at him!* Already, silly old Norbert had forgotten everything he had just remembered!

A little later on, he tried again. "It's only a reflection… It's only a reflection…" he muttered as he leaned his head over the trough, closed his eyes, and began to drink the clear, cold water. When his big fat belly was too full to drink any more, he drew his head back and frowned. He waited for the ripples in the water to die down and looked again.

Was it a trick of the light? Was he seeing things? No - there was no denying the awful truth…

NORBERT'S TEETH WERE GREEN!

"Oh Colin! Colin!" he whinnied as he arrived panting and wheezing beneath the old sycamore tree "My teeth are *green*!"

"Goodness me, Norbert," came the impatient reply from above "this is hardly front page news! Your teeth have *always* been green. It's what comes of a lifetime of chewing grass and never cleaning them. Now will you kindly trot along and leave me in peace whilst I finish my crossword."

"But what will Delilah think if she sees me?" Norbert pleaded. "Her teeth are always lovely and white!"

Delilah was a pretty young pony who sometimes grazed in the adjacent field. Ever since he had set eyes on her, Norbert had been deeply in love, though he had never plucked up the courage to tell her so.

"Delilah is much younger than you, Norbert, and the little girl from the farm grooms her and cleans her teeth before the horse shows each weekend," Colin clucked. "Anyway, I thought we'd agreed that you were going to forget about that frisky filly. You know what Kipling said about the female of the species, don't you?"

"No," came the honest reply.

"He said that that they were deadlier than the male. Trust me, my friend, that girl spells trouble with a capital 'T', and you would be well advised to steer well clear of her if I were you!"

Heartbroken, Norbert waddled away, his head filled with sad thoughts. *Colin was ever so clever and was always right about everything. He was just a fat old horse. A brainless, fat old, horse. Why on Earth would a pretty pony like Delilah ever be interested in him? Yes - he would listen to Colin's advice and do his best to forget about her. Deep down, however, Norbert feared that Delilah was just about the only thing in the world he simply couldn't forget about, however hard he tried.*

"At least I still have Colin for a friend," he murmured as he plodded away to a far corner of the field.

"And *don't* go thinking you can hang around with me, either," came a grouchy voice from high up in the branches of the old sycamore tree.

Chapter 2

"Colin? Are you there?" It was the next morning and Norbert was back in his favourite spot underneath the old sycamore tree.

"Yes?" chirruped a voice from above.

"I've been thinking..."

"Really Norbert? I must say I find that *very* hard to believe. Now, if you don't mind pushing along..."

"No Colin," Norbert replied doggedly. "It's *true*; I *have* been thinking, all night long."

There followed a great deal of rustling as the cuckoo made a clumsy descent through the branches of the tree. Seconds later, a beaky face poked itself out from among the foliage.

"Well?" the cuckoo clucked. "And what, pray tell, have you been thinking about? The meaning of life, perhaps? Or maybe you have solved the age old question as to the origins of the universe?"

Norbert hesitated. He had a strong suspicion that Colin was not going to like what he was about to say, but he was determined to say it anyway.

"Erm no," he cringed "not *exactly*. I've been thinking that I *would* like to clean my teeth. I know what you said about Delilah, but I still think that if I had clean teeth she *might* want to talk to me and we could become friends."

"Oh, you do, do you?"

"Yes."

Hopping down from his branch, Colin landed with a *plop* on the end of Norbert's nose and fixed him with a steely glare.

"And has it occurred to you by any chance that, in order to clean your teeth, you would need a toothbrush and some toothpaste?"

"Oh?" Norbert frowned. Indeed, this had not occurred to him…

"Of course you would," the cuckoo continued "and as you do not possess either of the above, we can safely say that the matter is concluded and that this nonsense must cease."

"Eh?"

"I am *trying* to explain to you that however much you want to clean your teeth, it simply isn't possible. Now – if you don't mind, I'll be heading home to finish the crossword I was doing before I was so rudely interrupted."

And with these words, Colin hopped from his perch on the horse's nose and set off on the short-haul flight back up to his nest.

Baffled, Norbert looked around in dismay. It was a beautiful morning, the bright sunshine warming his flanks, a gentle breeze tickling his tangled mane, making the dandelions dance along the bottom of the hedgerow. And yet at that moment, he felt sadder than he had ever done before in his whole life. Absent-mindedly, he wandered over to the five-bar gate that separated his field from Delilah's. There was no sign of her today; she must be away at a horse show - a good thing as he desperately didn't want her to see him while his teeth were still green. He was about to waddle back over to the water trough for another look at them when something truly astonishing occurred; Norbert had *another* thought! For almost an hour he stood motionless as, from tiniest grain in the back of his mind, this thought grew and grew, finally blossoming into a dazzling rainbow of hope that sent a shiver through his whole body. *At last!* For the first time *ever* in his life, Norbert had had an *idea*! But wait...this was more than just an idea... against all the odds, he had actually come up with a *plan*!

*

"Colin?"

"Yes Norbert?"

"I'm back."

"Yes – I gathered that. And how can I be of assistance?"

"I've been thinking again."

"Look! How many times do I have to tell you..."

"No Colin. I really have been thinking. I *am* going to clean my teeth but I need *you* to help me."

"Norbert *please* try and understand. You don't have a toothbrush or any toothpaste. Neither do I. Your owner, Farmer Finbar, is a mean and grumpy old so-and-so who would *never* in a million years think to give your teeth a clean. What's more, you are shut up in a field. The gate is closed and you can't possibly get out in order to obtain a toothbrush. And there I rest my case."

"But..."

"Goodbye, my friend – don't forget to write."

"But…"

"Farewell. Au revoir. Adios."

There followed what is sometimes referred to as a *pregnant* silence as Norbert pondered the situation.

"Colin?"

"Yes?"

"Can you fly?"

"Of *course* I can fly. What do you think I am? I'm a cuckoo, you know – not some species of penguin!"

"I was thinking that, if you can fly, then you could fly away and find a toothbrush and some toothpaste for me."

"That is the most *ridiculous* suggestion I have *ever* heard."

"But why?"

"Well...Well... I... I..."

Norbert peered up into the dense foliage, a glimmer of hope swelling in his heart. *If he could only persuade Colin to go along with his plan...*

"Farmer Finbar's house is just up on the hill over there. I can see that he has some of those window things open because it's such a hot day. You could easily fly in through one of them and borrow a toothbrush and some toothpaste for me."

"Oh – I could, could I?"

"Yes, Colin - you could."

For a moment, it was the cuckoo's turn to be baffled.

"Well I c… can't," he stammered. "I can't because... Because I'm feeling a little bit under the weather today and need to rest. Yes that's it – I need to rest. Awfully sorry about that, but there it is."

Norbert knew that it was now or never. *The moment had come for him to play his trump card.*

"If I had clean teeth and made friends with Delilah, I could talk to her every day and wouldn't need to disturb you again, ever."

A stunned silence from above.

"N... Not disturb me again?"

"No Colin."

"Ever?"

"No Colin."

"Let me get this straight, Norbert. You are saying that if I were somehow able to purloin a toothbrush and clean your teeth, allowing you to strike up a warm and loving friendship with Delilah, you would then be prepared to leave me alone? Forever?"

"Yes Colin."

"Forever and ever Amen?"

"Yes Colin."

"Right ho! Clear the runway – Standby for take-off - I'm coming down!"

Chapter 3

Colin's descent from the sycamore tree was a harrowing spectacle which did not bode well for the mission ahead. First there came a violent rustling sound from high up in the branches. This was immediately followed by a strangled 'squawk,' as something plump and feathery emerged from the foliage in a steep downward trajectory, hurtling like a meteor towards the ground below.

"Colin?"

"Yes?" came the winded reply.

"Are you *sure* you can fly?" Norbert stood peering down anxiously at his friend who was now lying in a crumpled heap between his front hooves.

"Of *course* I can fly!" Colin gasped. "Everyone knows that the cuckoo flies south each winter to enjoy the warming African sun."

Norbert shuffled his hooves uneasily. For as long as he could remember, Colin had spent every single winter in his nest in the sycamore tree, but he was worried that pointing this out would only make his feathered friend even angrier.

"Is it nice in Africa?" he ventured tactfully.

"Well... I must confess I haven't been down there for a year or two. It *is* a bit of a trek after all, and when you get to my age, it's important not to overdo these things. Anyway, enough of this chit-chat," he clucked, eager to change the subject as quickly as possible. "I have daring deeds to perform. Now stand aside while I prepare for take-off."

"Of course I can fly," said Colin. "Now stand aside while I prepare for take-off!"

Again, Norbert studied his friend with concern. Though Colin *was* unquestionably a cuckoo, a species of bird capable of flying thousands of miles each year, there was something about him that did not seem *quite* right. Whereas a fit and healthy cuckoo has a long, straight tail, Colin's was a crooked affair which seemed to stick out at a peculiar angle. And whilst a healthy cuckoo has pointed, streamlined wings like a fighter jet, Colin's looked tatty and misshapen, like a World War I bi-plane that has been machine-gunned from the trenches below.

"Maybe we should think of a different plan," Norbert began, but he was too late.

Ignoring his plea, the cuckoo suddenly lurched into motion and began to taxi unsteadily along a strip of flattened grass that was to serve as a runway. Norbert could only look on in growing alarm as his friend rapidly picked up speed before launching himself skywards with a strangled *squawk!* To his amazement, the plump cuckoo somehow managed to remain in the air, feverishly flapping his wings, pitching and wheeling wildly from side to side.

"Gug, gug , gug, gug!" Colin cried as he swooped high above the horse's head.

“Pardon?” Norbert replied, squinting up into the sunshine.

“It’s the sound that a cuckoo makes when agitated,” Colin explained “and believe me, I am *seriously* agitated right now. If I’m not back within the hour, please inform my next-of-kin that I perished nobly in the field of duty. I would like to request a quiet funeral ceremony with only close family present. No flowers please.”

And with these chilling words, he flew off in the direction of Finbar’s farmhouse. Norbert watched as his friend headed away into the distance until he became nothing more than a speck on the horizon. A plump, odd-looking speck, but a speck nonetheless.

Unsure about how to pass the time before his friend returned, Norbert lowered his head and began to munch away at a clump of long grass. He had barely finished his first mouthful when he paused. Growing ever-louder, he could hear a noise. It was a chugging, whirring sort of a noise; the sound of a motor car engine. Raising his head, he gazed across the fields to the old lane and was dismayed to see a car heading in his direction, towing what was clearly a small, pink horsebox.

“*Delilah,*” he gibbered despairingly “*and my teeth are still green!*”

He watched, transfixed, as the vehicle drew ever nearer, finally grinding to a halt by the gate of the adjacent field. Both car doors opened and a little girl hopped excitedly out of the passenger side, chatting happily to her father who emerged stiffly from the driver’s seat sporting a smart, green wax jacket. He had the air of a man who belonged in a suburban semi-detached house, but who enjoyed indulging his daughter’s hobby at weekends as this allowed him to briefly imagine himself in the role of a country Squire. They conversed for a few seconds before the man began to unfasten the sturdy metal catches that secured the door of the horse box. Norbert goggled in rapt wonder as, with the uncanny grace of a supermodel on a catwalk, Delilah trotted down the ramp towards her owner. Slimy green dribble dripped from Norbert’s lower lip as he watched the little girl gently stroking Delilah’s golden mane before giving her a carrot, closely followed by a sugar lump. Glancing at his watch, her father mumbled something about needing to be home in time for the football game on TV and so, having given Delilah another hug, the little girl hopped back into the car. Seconds later, there was a rumble of an engine and they were gone.

For a moment, Delilah stood and watched as the car disappeared into the distance. Norbert glanced around anxiously. He loved Delilah and *did* want to talk to her, but *not* until his teeth had been cleaned. Although she was in a different field, there was only a low hedge separating them, and he realized to his dismay that he would be clearly visible wherever he stood. There were some rather large badger holes down at the bottom of Finbar's field, near the pond, but he was fairly certain that he would not fit into any of these. Anyway, the badgers were notoriously grumpy old things and would not take kindly to a horse trying to join them their cosy set. Indeed, the only possible feature that offered any sort of cover was the sycamore tree. Though it was a very large tree with a wide trunk, Norbert was much too fat to fully conceal himself behind it, but it w0ould at least provide *a little* camouflage. *Yes! Delilah would never spot him there: he would stand still and silently beneath its leafy branches until Colin returned with the toothbrush and toothpaste.*

"Oh Norbert! Cooey!" came a musical voice from the gate of the next field. Delilah had immediately noticed his large rotund belly protruding around each side of the tree trunk. Panic-stricken, Norbert did the only thing he could think of, which was to pretend he hadn't heard her.

"Oh Noooooorbert!" she hollered, much louder this time. "Yoo hooo!"

Unable to ignore her any longer, Norbert raised his head and turned slowly towards the sound of her voice. Even from fifty yards away, he could clearly see the sun glinting off her dazzling white teeth.

"Hello Delilah." Norbert spoke like a bad ventriloquist, moving his lips as little as possible lest she should catch a glimpse of his mouldy molars.

Delilah was puzzled, if not a little offended. Usually Norbert would trot across to talk to her as soon as she came home. *Had he gone off her? Had he fallen for another filly?*

Norbert needed to think quickly. Unfortunately, thinking quickly was not one of his strongest points.

"Why don't you come over to the gate?" Delilah whinnied happily, craning her neck as far as she could over into Norbert's field. "Then we can catch up without having to shout at the top of our voices."

Norbert began to panic.

"I've erm... I've got a bit of a sore leg today," he cringed "so I think it's best if I stay over here for the time being."

The distance between the two horses, combined with Norbert's determination not to reveal even a glimpse of his teeth rendered his feeble excuse completely unintelligible to Delilah.

"I *do* wish you wouldn't mumble so, Norbert. I'm only trying to be friendly, but if you don't want to see me, then you can suit yourself, old misery guts!" she snapped before turning and cantering off to the furthest end of her field in a huff.

Chapter 4

Meanwhile, up at Finbar's farmhouse, Colin had alighted silently on the roof of the front porch and was busy carrying out a detailed reconnaissance of the enemy terrain. At least, this was the version of events that he later gave to Norbert when recounting his daring deeds to the gullible horse. In truth, he had flown hurtling and out of control towards the house and had struck a pane of glass in the porch doorway with an almighty *thump.* Rendered completely senseless by the collision, he had then proceeded to drop like a brick onto the concrete doorstep where he reposed lifelessly for almost half-an-hour, his stumpy yellow legs sticking straight up in the air. When he came to, it took him a further fifteen minutes to remember who he was, where he was, and why he was there.

Little did Colin know that this was merely the beginning of the multiple misfortunes that fate had in store for him that day. Tragically, he had chosen to undertake his heroic mission on a Friday. Friday, alas, just happened to be the day when, after a hard week's work, Farmer Finbar liked to take a long, hot soak in the bathtub. Like many people, Finbar kept his bathtub in the bathroom, the *very same* room that housed his toothbrush and toothpaste.

"Aaaaaaaah," the farmer grunted contentedly as he lowered his bulky frame into the warm, bubbly water. A grubby individual at the best of times, Finbar had earlier that morning cleaned out both the henhouse *and* the pigsty, and for this reason he was *even* dirtier and smellier than normal. For some moments he lay in a state of bliss, wallowing like a pink walrus in the hot suds, a large flannel draped over his face, his fat belly protruding like a small island above the frothy surface of the water as he dreamed happy dreams about a string of sausages in the fridge downstairs that he had earmarked for his supper. Then came the noise…

It was a light, fluttering, flapping kind of noise, and it came from the vicinity of the open window. For a split second, Farmer Finbar froze, still and silent, largely submerged beneath the soapy suds. Then came another flutter. And another. Very slowly, his heart beating like a drum, he peeled the flannel back from his bright red face, and what he saw almost made his piggy eyes start from their sockets.

"Very slowly, his heart beating like a drum, Finbar peeled the flannel back from his bright red face, and what he saw almost made his piggy eyes start from their sockets."

There was a bird... A bird in his bathroom! Nay – not just any bird... It looked like a cuckoo... A fat cuckoo! Goodness me - there was a fat cuckoo in his bathroom! He continued to goggle in silent amazement. *What was it doing now? It was using its beak to remove his toothbrush from the china pot on the sink...* His mouth agape, Finbar watched as the bird proceeded to flutter back across to the window and drop his toothbrush out on to the ground below before repeating the procedure with his tube of toothpaste.

So absorbed was Colin in his task that he was completely unaware of the danger that lurked beneath the soapy suds, and it thus came as a nasty shock when, from the vicinity of the bathtub in the corner of the room there came an almighty roar.

"GARN!" Finbar bellowed as he emerged from the bathwater like a Kraken from the deep. Soap-suds poured like a waterfall from his enormous belly, his face bright purple with rage as he clambered clumsily out onto the bathmat.

"*GAAAAARN*!" he roared again, as if to emphasize his point.

"Gug, gug , gug, gug!" Colin retorted as he flapped and fluttered around the ceiling of the bathroom, frantically trying to navigate his way towards the open window.

You may recall from earlier in the story, reader, that *gug, gug, gug, gug* is the sound that a cuckoo makes when agitated; I think we can all agree that there are few things more likely to induce a state of agitation than being chased around a bathroom by a naked farmer who is brandishing a loofah and who is clearly intent on using it to mash you into a sort of jelly. Such was Colin's terror as he swooped and dived that he accidentally emitted a runny pellet of cuckoo droppings which struck Finbar squarely on the forehead with a loud *splat!*

"*GAAARN*!" the farmer bawled, lashing out ever more furiously with the loofah, forcing Colin to retreat into a corner of the room away from the window that offered his route to salvation. But it was in this very moment, this darkest hour when all hope seemed lost, that Lady Luck seemed to smile down on the beleaguered cuckoo. For it was now, just as Finbar was preparing to close in for the kill, that the gooey white bird droppings began to dribble down the farmer's forehead and into his eyes, temporarily blinding him. Seizing his opportunity, Colin skimmed past his deadly foe with a gleeful *gug, gug, gug, gug* and made for the open window. Rubbing his eyes and seeing his prey slipping from his grasp, Finbar made a final desperate lunge with the loofah, almost losing his balance as he did so. As he charged like a bull towards the window, he then suffered the final indignity of stepping on a bar of soap, upon which he performed what appeared to be an elaborate double pirouette on the wet, soapy tiles, before going to ground with a sickening *CRUMP*, clipping his forehead on the corner of the sink as he went down.

"Garn!" he muttered feebly as his world faded into blackness.

Chapter 5

As the sun moved steadily westwards across the sky, Norbert once again found himself standing beneath the leafy canopy of the old sycamore tree. Pondering the events of the last few hours, it seemed that he *must* be daydreaming. In the hedge that bordered the field, a host of sparrows were chitter-chattering busily among themselves in preparation for bedtime. Under normal circumstances, Norbert found these noisy little birds particularly irritating, but not today. Indeed, he did not even mind when a big hairy blue-bottle alighted on his nose and took a short stroll up his face and across his eyeball, such was his state of deepest bliss. Because today was the day when his teeth had finally been cleaned! In his long and uneventful life, he could not recall a time when he had ever felt happier.

Earlier that afternoon, things had been very different. Having watched Colin setting out on his daring mission, Norbert had been driven close to despair when, after more than an hour, there was no sign of his return. Then a speck had emerged into view on the horizon. A plump, odd-looking speck. As the speck drew nearer, Norbert could see that it was clutching something in its beak. *A toothbrush! But wait... The speck appeared to have dropped the toothbrush in a field of corn... Oh no! But what was this? The speck was diving down to retrieve it...*

When Colin finally *had* made it back to the sycamore tree and dropped the toothbrush between his friend's hooves, Norbert had studied it doubtfully. It didn't seem to have very many bristles left, and the few that remained were badly discoloured, having been used twice daily by Farmer Finbar over a period of several years, but it was still a toothbrush of sorts and would have to do.

"But what about the..." Norbert had begun, his voice bursting with anxiety.

"The toothpaste? Yes - I know!" Colin had clucked breathlessly, visibly distressed.

"I couldn't carry both, so I'm now going to have to go all the way back to Finbar's farm to get it! I did manage to drop it out of the window, so at least I will not need to risk a further foray into the Bathroom of Terror."

"Bathroom of Terror?"

"Yes. It's how I shall be referring to the bathroom at Finbar's farm from now on."

"Oh – I see."

"Now clear the runway for take-off."

Twenty minutes later, Colin had returned carrying the tube of toothpaste, looking even more haggard than before. He had, he explained, only narrowly survived an encounter with Farmer Finbar's cat, Jasper, whilst retrieving the tube from its resting place beneath the bathroom window. Norbert had noted with some sympathy that his friend appeared to have considerably fewer tail feathers than he had possessed at the outset of his mission.

If I told you that the tooth-cleaning process had been straightforward, I would be leading you astray. Indeed, it was fraught with difficulty, largely due to the fact that neither Norbert (being a horse) nor Colin (being a cuckoo) possessed anything that could accurately be described as 'hands'. Next time you clean your teeth, try doing so without using your hands and you will gain some understanding of the sheer enormity of the task that confronted the two friends on that sunny afternoon in May.

Over a period of several hours, they tried and tested innumerable schemes and stratagems in a bid to clean Norbert's teeth, each failing to produce the desired results. There is a well-known saying that states "*If at first you don't succeed, try, try and try again.*" Norbert and Colin had never heard this saying, but nevertheless they tried, tried and tried again. And again. And again.

To describe the final method whereby they finally *did* manage to clean Norbert's teeth would require several very long and complicated chapters, so I shall merely mention that it involved the use of a plank of wood, a piece of barbed wire, nine hedge-sparrows, a rusty baked-bean tin, a length of old rope and an extremely unhappy badger.

Well reader - work it out for yourself...

Chapter 6

It was with a mixture of excitement and trepidation that Norbert approached the trough in order to study his reflection. Colin had assured him that his teeth *were* clean, but cuckoos are not always the best judges in matters of dental hygiene.

His friend had long since retired to his nest, high up in the branches of the old sycamore tree. The whole affair had undoubtedly taken its toll on the ageing bird and the loud snoring sounds from up in the dense foliage were drifting far and wide, carried across the fields on the gentle May breeze. Otherwise, apart from the occasional buzzing of a bumble bee going about his daily chores, all was quiet in Finbar's Field.

Norbert turned his gaze across to Delilah's paddock. She appeared to have forgotten about their earlier unpleasant exchange, and was now standing in a sunny spot close to the five bar gate that separated their fields.

This was it - the moment of truth! The moment upon which his entire future would depend!

Squinting at the shimmering surface of the water, Norbert leaned over the trough and drew back his pink, rubbery lips. He blinked. And blinked again... *It could not be... Or could it? Yes – the truth was undeniable....*

NORBERT'S TEETH WERE WHITE!

Some people believe that a horse's face is not capable of expressing emotions or feelings; these people are wrong. Norbert's face as he trotted across the field towards the five bar gate where Delilah awaited him was every bit as expressive as that of any human being. Indeed, it could be said that he grinned like no horse had ever grinned before. There are, of course, different types of grins. There are cheeky grins; there are friendly grins; there are crafty grins. Unfortunately for Norbert, *his* grin resembled that of a raving lunatic, his lips pulled right back over his teeth, the sheer concentration required to maintain his bizarre expression leaving him cross-eyed.

"Hi Norbert!" Delilah called brightly, noticing his waddling approach. "So you've decided to come and see me after all. I was just wondering if you fancied... Oh..." She stopped mid-sentence, gaping at the dazzling dentures on display before her, Norbert looking on in dismay and confusion as the smile froze on Delilah's face and then vanished.

"Oh Norbert! How *could* you?" she squealed.

"B... B... But... I...I thought..."

"Look at your teeth! They're *white*!"

"Y...Yes...Well I just thought..."

"You thought you would show me up didn't you? By having teeth that were whiter than mine! How *dare* you! I shall *never, ever* speak to you again!"

And with these words, she turned and galloped furiously away to the farthest corner of her field.

For several minutes, Norbert stood as still as a statue before turning and waddling back to his favourite spot in the shade of the old sycamore tree.

"Are you awake Colin?" he whinnied sadly.

"I am now, Norbert."

The cuckoo listened in rapt horror as the full details of the difficult encounter with Delilah were relayed to him.

"But things could always be worse, Colin," Norbert ended with rising optimism in his voice.

"How do you mean?" came the suspicious reply.

"Well – at least I still have one friend...YOU!"

There was a lengthy pause, followed by a *gug, gug, gug, gug* so loud that it could be heard in several adjoining counties.

This, reader, in case you have forgotten, is the sound that a cuckoo makes when agitated.

Epilogue

Farmer Finbar awoke with a shiver. *Where was he?* It was pitch dark and he was lying on a cold, hard floor in a puddle of soapy water. His head throbbed as he tried in vain to piece together the events of the day. Rising unsteadily, he groped around the walls for the light switch, wincing in agony as the bright strip light on the bathroom ceiling illuminated the room. *What had happened? Had he been drinking a little too much home-made cider again?* He reeled a little, clutching at the sink for support. Gripping the porcelain firmly with both hands to steady himself, it occurred to him that there was something different about the sink. Something that was usually there, but which had mysteriously disappeared. *What could it be?* Then came the realisation: *his toothbrush and toothpaste were missing!* He blinked twice and splashed a little cold water on his face. Slowly but surely as his thoughts unscrambled, the high drama that had earlier unfolded in that very room came flooding back to him... *There had been a bird... A cuckoo... No... It had been a FAT cuckoo... In his bathroom, stealing his toothbrush and toothpaste. But no... That was surely impossible... Cuckoos stealing dental products? That just didn't happen... Or did it?*

"Sometimes I wonder if you're losing your marbles, Finbar," he muttered as he turned to head for the bedroom. "You must have taken that there toothbrush downstairs without meaning to. That bump on the head is making your memory play tricks on you, I reckon."

Half way to the bathroom door, he stopped. There was something stuck to the sole of his foot. In his heart of hearts, Finbar knew immediately what it was, but hardly dared to look. Still dazed, half wondering whether he was still in the middle of a bad dream, he stooped down and peeled the object from his foot.

"*GARN!*" he cried, goggling in utter disbelief. For there in the palm of his hand, soggy, grey and crooked, but unmistakable nonetheless, lay a feather. A feather that looked suspiciously like it might have once belonged to a fat cuckoo...

The End

Roger the Frog

Chapter 1

Now then reader, are you sitting comfortably? Or are you tucked up in your bed? You might even be lying on a tropical beach or standing on top of a windy mountain. Perhaps you are hiding deep in the Amazon rainforest, or simply snuggled in the back seat of a car... Wherever you happen to be, I must urge you to relax and rid your mind of all the distractions of the outside world so that you may lend your full concentration to the strange and tragic tale that I am about to relate. Are you ready? You are sure that you don't need to go to the toilet or anything? Very well - hold on a second while clear my throat... Hrrrrrrgh! There... that's better – away we go!

Roger the frog sat on his lily pad and thought about his life. And the more he thought about his life, the more unhappy Roger became. He had lived in this particular pond since the day he was spawned, together with his mother, Freda, his father, Frank, and his two older sisters, Florence and Felicity. For reasons he did not fully understand, Roger had always felt *different* somehow, as though he was the odd one out. Weeks and months of misery and boredom passed by until one day, he decided that enough was enough; today would be the day that he would venture forth into the Big Wide World so that his life might begin anew. At long last, Roger vowed, he was going to *be* something.

"Father?" he croaked, peering anxiously into the dense thicket of bulrushes that surrounded the pond. "Are you there?"

"Of *course* I am," Father replied, emerging into the spring sunshine and taking his place on the lily pad adjacent to his son's. Father's lily pad was an especially sturdy affair; it had to be, as he was especially large for a frog and extremely fat. "You know very well that I've never, ever left the pond in my whole life."

"That's what I wanted to talk to you about," Roger sighed. "I have never left this pond either and I was wondering..."

"Of *course* you haven't, my dear boy!" Father exclaimed. "It may surprise you to learn that your Grandfather never left the pond either. Indeed, legend has it that *his* father also stayed put. Which leads me on to your Grandfather's Father's Father. Now, he was a fine fellow who went by the name of Fernando, and do you know what?"

"*He* never left the pond either?"

"Good Lord! However did you guess?"

"Please, Father!" Roger wailed. "I can't stand it anymore!"

"My dear boy! What*ever* is the matter?"

"It's this lily pad, Father, this *pond*!"

"What do you mean, Roger? It's a very nice lily pad – the most comfortable in the whole pond apart from mine, your mother's and those belonging to your two sisters."

"But Father! Have you never dreamed of the Big Wide World beyond?"

"*A world beyond the pond?*" the aged amphibian eyed his son with growing alarm. "Calm down, my dear boy – this is dangerous talk! You must never let your mother hear you speak of such things."

"What things?" The voice was that of Freda, Roger's mother.

Recognising her deep, rasping baritone, Roger spun round on his lily pad. Although she was relatively small in stature, Freda had the personality of a belligerent alligator and she thus ruled the pond and all who dwelt within it with a rod of iron.

"Hello Dearest," Frank gulped nervously. "Roger and I were just talking about our proud family history. How, for generation after generation, no frog in our family has *ever* left this pond."

"Correct." Freda replied with an air of undisguised menace. "And what of it?"

"Roger was just saying he felt a little restless, Darling." Father squirmed.

"*Restless?*"

"I... I'm sorry Mother," Roger stammered. "I was just talking to Father about the pond and my lily pad and I was w... wondering whether a change of scene might do me good."

"A change of scene?"

"Yes Mother."

"Might do you good?"

"Yes Mother."

"I see." And with these words, she fell silent. On their respective lily pads, Roger and his father trembled. Each knew that whenever Mother fell silent, serious trouble would inevitably follow.

Roger quivered. Roger quailed. A keen observer would probably have noticed that he quaked a little too. *I must not speak, I must not speak, I must not speak* he repeated over and over to himself in his head. It was not long, however (for Roger was a weak-minded individual, even for a frog) before the tension became too much to bear.

"The *food!"* he blurted.

"I *beg* your pardon?" Mother growled.

"The food!" the poor frog repeated, his voice cracking with emotion. "I can't *stand* it anymore!"

"Well, of all the ungrateful..."

"But Mother – surely you cannot enjoy eating nothing but flies, worms and slugs each and every day!"

"I have *never* heard such insolence!"

Roger, perhaps believing that he had already sealed his doom and thus had nothing to lose, carried on regardless.

"I am *sick and tired* of flies Mother! *Surely* you must understand!"

"*Nonsense!*" Freda snarled.

"Mother – *please*!" the young frog gibbered. "Tell me this: what was it that we had for lunch yesterday?"

"Yesterday was Wednesday. You know full well that we always have flies on a Wednesday."

"And for tea?"

"For tea? Why – I do believe we had flies."

"And finally, Mother," Roger sobbed, "tell me what it was that we had for breakfast this morning."

Freda drew herself up to her full height, puffing out her throat in defiance. She was not accustomed to such emotional outbursts from her son.

"If I remember correctly," she replied in a low, threatening voice, "we had flies."

"Ha!" Roger cried triumphantly. "Do you not see what I'm getting at?"

"My dear boy," Father cut in, sensing that intervention of some sort was needed before the situation turned ugly. "You mother and I have only ever acted in your best interests: flies are very nutritious. Besides, we always thought you *liked* flies."

"*Like* them? I *hate* them!"

"We could always have slugs on a Wednesday if it will make things any better..."

"Father! Mother!" Roger looked sadly from one parent to the other. "You have always been kind to me. I know I have never been the son you hoped for and that you always favoured your daughters, Florence and Felicity..."

"Correct," they chimed in unison.

"But I am afraid that I have made my decision."

"Oh?"

"Yes," Roger gurgled, big salty tears forming in his eyes. "I am leaving. There *must* be more to life than flies! There *must* be a world beyond the pond. I want to make something of myself, to *be* something! Please do not shed any tears on my account – God willing I shall return someday, triumphant..."

"Ok - Goodbye then," Mother waved him off cheerfully. "I'm sorry Roger, but I need to be getting on with preparing lunch. I thought we'd have flies for a change. Frank – tell Florence and Felicity it will be ready in an hour."

Chapter 2

As Roger hopped away, his tiny brain fizzed with bitter thoughts. *Typical parents! They could at least have pretended that they were sorry to see him go! Where WAS he going anyway?*

Alone and afraid, the little frog peered around in an effort to get his bearings. The pond, he noted, was situated in the bottom corner of a large, sloping field. In the centre of the field, there stood an enormous tree, beneath which there lurked what appeared to be a gigantic monster. Roger's eyes bulged as he studied its colossal form; *never had he imagined in his wildest dreams that the Big Wide World could contain such a fearsome creature...* And yet, the poor frog realized, he had little choice but to make his way stealthily up the hill towards it; the only alternative was to head back down to the dreaded pond, his parents and his wretched lily pad.

I'd rather be eaten by a terrible monster than face that he pondered miserably. *Besides, I am but a small frog – If I am lucky, perhaps I shall be able to sneak past without him noticing....*

Summoning all of the bravery he could muster, Roger hopped onwards. And then he hopped again. He was in the process of limbering up for a third hop when something brown and spindly danced across his path. Mesmerized, Roger followed the strange creature with his beady eyes as it fluttered back and forth in front of him.

"Hello," said Roger.

"Hello," replied the *thing*. It spoke in a weedy, whiny little voice.

"I *do* wish you would keep still," Roger pleaded, his eyes rolling in their sockets as he struggled to keep up with the creature's movements.

"Keep still? Can't keep still!" it buzzed. "I'm dancing!"

"Dancing?" As he studied his new acquaintance more closely, Roger could see it had wings and that its face bore an uncanny resemblance to that of a fly. And yet this creature was quite unlike any other fly he had previously encountered. Firstly, its body was long and thin, in stark contrast to the fat, juicy specimens that Mother gave him for breakfast, lunch and tea each day.

More startling still were its legs - to merely describe them as *long* would be a gross understatement; the legs belonging to the creature that danced before him were *outrageous*! Indeed, they were of such a length that it appeared to be teetering on a pair of oversized stilts.

"What kind of creature are you?" he enquired in a kind of hushed awe.

"*Officially*, we are referred to as the *crane fly*," it replied in its reedy tones "but most of the time people tend to call us by our nickname..."

"Oh?"

"Yes, my dear friend," the creature buzzed with a hint of pride. "You are looking at a perfect example of what is commonly known as a *Daddy Longlegs*."

"Gosh!" Roger croaked, deeply impressed. "Do you do anything else apart from dancing?"

"Of course not! We Daddy Longlegs' are, if you'll pardon the expression, *born to boogie*."

"Gosh! It sounds like you have *much* more fun than we frogs. Do you think *I* could become a Daddy Longlegs one day?"

"Mmmm," the insect sniffed, looking Roger up and down disapprovingly. "You're a bit of a slimy fellow, aren't you?"

"Slimy? But..."

"And a little overweight..."

"*Overweight*? Now just you hold on a minute..."

"But all things considered, I don't see any reason why you wouldn't make a perfectly good Daddy Longlegs."

"Great!" Roger beamed foolishly. "When can I start?"

"Why, you can start right away. Come on – let me see your moves..."

"My moves?"

"Your *dance* moves, silly! If you want to be a dancer, you need to have some moves – the funkier the better."

"Well... I'm not sure that I..."

"Come on! How about a simple salsa to start things off?"

Poor Roger looked around, desperately seeking a way out of his predicament. He had never danced before; there simply wasn't much call for it in the pond, and he now feared that his lack of experience would be brutally exposed. He was considering making up an excuse about his ankle being a bit sore when his parting words to Mother and Father flashed into his mind: *I want to make something of myself, to be something* he had proclaimed. At that moment, Roger resolved that, whatever happened, there would be no going back.

"Ok," he gulped. "I'll give it a go."

Have you ever seen a frog attempting to do the salsa? If you haven't, you may consider yourself lucky; were you ever to bump into this particular Daddy Longlegs, he would undoubtedly confirm that frogs make truly *terrible* dancers. The problem is that their long, ungainly hind legs, feeble front limbs and fat little bellies combine to severely restrict their rhythmic movement. Whilst Roger could not be faulted for effort, wiggling his bottom and jerking his little forelimbs for all he was worth, the frog as a species is simply not designed to do justice to a style as demanding as the salsa.

"Bravo!" the Daddy Longlegs applauded as Roger, panting with exhaustion, brought his random jiggling to its sorry conclusion. Fortunately, he was a kindly soul and was able to largely conceal his dismay at the ghastly spectacle he had just witnessed.

"That wasn't bad. Not bad at all..."

"Really?" The frog wheezed, unable to conceal his surprise.

"Really," the insect lied. "There's always room for improvement, of course, but I truly believe that, with a little careful tuition, you will make a fine Daddy Longlegs."

"Oh joy of joys!" Roger cried triumphantly. "At *last*, I am going to *be* something! Wait until I tell Mother and Father!"

The Daddy Longlegs took to the air and began to buzz away in an easterly direction, motioning for Roger to follow. "Come on – there's a whole host of my friends dancing around in the next field if you'd care to join us."

"Oh yes!" the frog whooped, hopping up and down on the spot with delight. "Of course I will – why, it must almost be time for lunch."

"Lunch?"

"Yes, lunch." There was something about the insect's manner that sent an uneasy chill down Roger's spine. "I forgot to ask," he continued. "What is it that you fellows eat again?"

"Eat?" the Daddy Longlegs laughed. "We don't really bother with eating – there simply isn't time, what with all of our dancing commitments."

"But you *must* eat," Roger gulped, growing more alarmed with each passing second. "You must eat in order to *survive*."

"Survive?" the insect giggled as though his new friend had said something truly bizarre. "My dear fellow – we Daddy Longlegs' don't have time to think about things like *surviving*!"

"Oh?"

"Why, no – of *course* not! We are born, we dance around for a bit, we find a mate and have babies..."

"Oh?"

"And then a couple of weeks after that, we die. Now come along – we're going to miss out on all the fun at this rate."

"H... Hold on a second," the poor frog stammered. "Did you just say that you only live for a couple of weeks and then you die?"

"Of *course* we do! Every last one of us!"

"You might have mentioned that in the first place."

"I'm terribly sorry – must have slipped my mind. Didn't think it mattered, you see..."

"*You didn't think it mattered?* Two weeks doesn't seem very long to me..."

"All the more reason why we must get the dancing underway without further ado!"

"I... I'm sorry," Roger whimpered. "But I've changed my mind. I don't think I want to be a Daddy Longlegs anymore..."

"Oh well – suit yourself. It's a wonderful life while it lasts, you know." And with these words, the creature buzzed its wings and flitted away to join its pals in the next field, zigging and zagging as it went.

Roger watched it go with a mixture of sadness and relief before, with a hop and a wriggle and a wriggle and a hop, he continued on his way.

Chapter 3

Roger had not travelled more than a few yards through the long grass before he came face to face with *another* strange creature. This time, the newcomer was a furry specimen with a pointy, devious-looking face and overly-prominent front teeth.

"Get out of my way!" it squeaked.

"I *beg your pardon*?" Roger rejoined haughtily, puffing out his throat with indignation. Mother and Father had their faults but at least they had taught him basic manners.

"Get out of my way, I say!" the creature squeaked again, even more shrilly than before.

"What a rude little fellow you are!" the frog retorted.

"How *dare* you call me rude? How *rude* of you!"

"*I* wasn't being rude. *You* were the one who was being rude to *me!*"

"No I *wasn't*!"

"Yes you *were!*"

"No I was *not*!"

"Yes you *were!*"

“No I was *not*!”

“Yes you *were!*”

“No I was *not*!”

Here the two creatures paused, each probing his adversary with beady eyes for any signs of weakness. Roger, for his part, was relieved to note that his enemy was, if anything, even smaller than he, thus affording him a decent chance of putting up a stout defence should the need arise.

“It would appear that we have reached an *impasse*,” Roger spoke defiantly, glaring at his whiskery foe for all he was worth.

“What the *devil* are you talking about? Stand aside, I say!”

“It’s a phrase that the French use to describe a situation where further progress for either party is impossible.”

“Well - if you put it like that, I suppose you’re right.”

“What kind of creature are you, anyway?” Roger enquired, sensing that he was gaining the upper hand in the negotiations.

“I am a mouse,” it replied. “I go by the name of Miguel.”

“I am a frog,” Roger spoke calmly. “I go by the name of Roger.”

“That’s a silly name for a frog.”

"You are entitled to your opinion, however, I, for one, do not intend to lower myself to engage in the hurling of childish insults."

"Stinky bum!"

"Now listen here, you vulgar little fiend," Roger croaked in his sternest voice. "I have set out on a noble journey to explore the Big Wide World..."

"*Stinky bum!*"

"I intend to proceed on my way and am determined that nothing shall stop me."

"*Stinky bum!*"

"So if you don't mind, you can step aside and let me pass."

"*Shan't!*"

"My dear fellow – this is a big, wide field with plenty of room for both of us. Surely you can see that if you move to one side, we can both go about our business unhindered."

"*Shan't!* Why don't *you* step aside? It's *my* path, anyway."

"Your path?"

"Yes – we mice made this little path so it would be easier for us to scamper through the long grass."

"Oh – I see." This new information caught Roger off guard. *Perhaps the mouse had right of way after all.* "Where are you going, anyway?" he said, skilfully changing the subject.

"I've just been up to the farmhouse on the hill for some lunch."

"Lunch?" Roger's fat little belly gurgled at the very mention of the word.

"Yes," the mouse grinned, warming to the subject. "I tend to trickle up there around lunchtime most days. The chap who lives there, Farmer Finbar, is a greedy, messy old devil and there are always plenty of crumbs lying around on the kitchen floor."

"Crumbs?"

"Yes – biscuit crumbs, bread crumbs, cake crumbs, all kind of crumbs really."

"Gosh!" Roger drooled, a tiny rivulet of saliva dribbling down his chin. "It sounds like a wonderful life you have."

"It's not *too* bad, I suppose," Miguel conceded. "Now, if you don't mind, I'm just heading back to my cosy nest for an afternoon nap." And with these words, he nimbly skipped past Roger and scurried away down the path.

"Wait!" the frog cried. "Hold on a second, will you?"

Miguel stopped in his tracks; there was something about the sheer desperation in Roger's voice that tugged at his heart strings.

"What is it now?" he squeaked.

"Please," Roger implored. "I have left my home, my parents and my old life as a frog behind me so that I might *be* something. Do you think I could ever be a mouse?"

"Mmmm," Miguel scratched his chin thoughtfully. "You're a bit on the slimy side, aren't you?"

"Slimy? But..."

"And a little overweight..."

"*Overweight*? Well perhaps I *have* let myself go a little but..."

"But I suppose you *might* make a reasonable enough mouse. If you're prepared to put the work in, of course..."

"Oh joy of joys!" Roger squealed triumphantly. "Wait until I tell Mother and Father! Now then – about those crumbs..."

"What about them?"

"Why, you must take me to the farmhouse right away so that I may have my fill and thus begin my new life as a mouse!"

"Ok – I like your enthusiasm and there are plenty of crumbs for the two of us, so I suppose I'll take you there."

"Hurrah!"

"Follow me – just remember to keep low and watch out for predators."

Roger's face fell.

"Predators?" he quivered. "What you mean, *predators*?"

"You know," Miguel looked him steadily in the eye, grinning a toothy grin. "Predators – all those creatures that like to gobble up mice like us for their supper."

"Oh?"

"Yes – I've always said that the only drawback about being a mouse is the sheer number of predators we have."

"Well you might have mentioned it to me before I agreed to become one!" Roger gibbered, a cold shiver coursing down his spine. "What kind of predators are you talking about, anyway?"

"Well, there are the weasels for a start."

"Weasels?"

"Yes – and the stoats are almost as bad."

"Stoats?"

"Not to mention the owls, hawks and buzzards."

"B... B... Buzzards..."

"And the foxes are just a *nightmare.* And then, of course, there are the badgers. Cats are pretty deadly too, never mind the mink and the snakes..."

"M... M... Mink? S... S... Snakes?" Roger's eyes were by now bulging from their sockets in terror. "Miguel?"

"Yes? My dear fellow – what on Earth is wrong with you? You're looking rather pale all of a sudden? Is there something the matter?"

"I've changed my mind; I do not wish to be a mouse anymore."

Chapter 4

It was with a slightly sinking feeling in his heart that Roger continued on his noble quest. Twice he had encountered creatures whose lives had, on the surface, seemed so much more exciting than his own; on each occasion, he had discovered a sinister detail at the very last moment, only saving himself from a ghastly fate by the narrowest of margins. Though Roger was still as determined as ever to prove himself to Mother and Father, a niggling seed of doubt had been sown in the back of his miniscule mind; *was pond life really that bad after all?*

As he stalked his way onwards up the field through the long grass, he became aware of a persistent and alarming sound up ahead that grew ever louder as he approached; *the monster!* Roger stopped. Roger listened.

CHOMP, CHOMP, CHOMP went the terrible noise. Roger trembled.

MUNCH, MUNCH, MUNCH it continued. Roger trembled some more.

"Goodness me!" he gasped under his breath. *"It is eating the Earth! The monster is eating the Big Wide World!"*

Suddenly, he felt the ground shake beneath his feet; *the colossus was moving towards him! He would surely be devoured! What a tragic way to end a promising young life...*

Whimpering like a baby, Roger curled up into a ball, covering his eyes with his slimy little hands and awaited the end.

"Hello," thundered a big deep voice from somewhere up in the heavens.

"Flibble!" Roger replied, the sheer terror of the moment having deprived him of the power of coherent speech.

"Pardon?" the voice boomed. Though it was very deep and extremely loud, it had a gentle, soothing tone. It occurred to Roger for the first time that perhaps the beast did not mean him any harm after all. Still shaking, he blinked open a single beady eye and peeped out from between his fingers.

"I said 'flibble'," he confirmed in his bravest voice.

"Yes - I thought that was what you said." With growing curiosity, the creature lowered its enormous head to in order to examine its new acquaintance.

"I say!" Roger bleated as the enormous mouth drew closer, sending a rush of hot breath coursing over his skin like a Saharan wind. "Do you mind? We frogs are amphibians you know and need to keep our skin moist at all times."

"I'm sorry," the gentle voice replied. "I didn't know that you were a frog."

"I'm afraid I am," Roger sighed "though I hope to be something else one day."

"Oh?"

"Yes," the frog continued. "I'm afraid a frog's life is very boring indeed. Why - I'd rather be a monster like you than a frog any day!"

"A monster?" the voice laughed. "I'm not a monster!"

"Not a monster?"

"No – of course not."

"You're quite certain?"

"Yes."

"What are you then?"

"My name is Norbert. I am a horse."

"Gosh!" Roger quivered with awe. "A horse! I have heard of such things, but never in my wildest dreams did I ever think I would meet one!"

Norbert smiled one of his biggest horsey smiles. His life was generally a dull and lonely affair; largely ignored by his owner, Farmer Finbar, his only company was an ageing and generally irritable cuckoo named Colin who lived high up in the branches of the sycamore tree which stood in the middle of the field. It made a nice change to find someone who seemed pleased to meet him.

Roger, for his part, was not merely pleased to meet Norbert; he was *delighted. How silly he had been to even consider a career as a Daddy Longlegs or a mouse!* In that split second it became strikingly clear to Roger where his future lay; he would be a horse...

"Where are you going?" Norbert asked, flaring his huge nostrils.

"Oh, nowhere in particular," the frog replied. "I'm just heading out into the Big Wide World so that I might *be* something."

"Gosh!" the horse whinnied. "That sounds exciting."

"Yes – it is rather. As a matter of fact," Roger continued, puffing out his chest with pride "I've more or less decided that I would like to be a horse."

This came as something of a surprise to Norbert. Though he had never been the most intelligent of animals, there was something about the idea of a frog declaring its intention to become a horse that seemed rather odd.

"Are you sure you're going to be a horse?" he ventured.

"Of *course* I am!" Roger clucked testily. "I see no reason why not. Do you?

"W... Well I was just thinking..."

"What, precisely were you thinking?"

"I was just thinking that perhaps you're a bit..." Resting his gaze on the plump, slimy little creature nestling deep down in the long grass, Norbert struggled to find the right words.

"A bit what?"

"A bit... *small.*"

"*Small*?" Roger huffed, puffing out his throat with indignation. "I've never heard such rot! We frogs *can* grow, you know!"

Norbert frowned. Even with his throat puffed out, the frog still somehow lacked the stature of a horse. A squashed tennis ball – yes. A horse – definitely not.

"And what is more," Roger continued, "anyone with half a brain knows that size isn't everything. Oh yes, my friend – I'm sure that there's a lot more to being a horse than simply being large."

"Oh?"

"Of *course* there is! Why, to be a good horse, one has to... to..." Here the foolish frog faltered as it occurred to him for the first time that he hadn't the faintest idea what one had to do in order to be considered a good horse. "What *exactly* is it that you fellows do, incidentally?"

Now, reader – you and I both know that, as a species, horses can be blessed with great beauty and majesty, a living, breathing symbol of freedom and purity, their bodies, flawless wonders of evolution, capable of galloping at terrific speeds and leaping enormous hurdles. Norbert, alas, was *not* this kind of a horse. If I were to tell you that Norbert was fat, lazy and dim-witted, I would be leading you astray; Norbert was *extremely* fat, *extremely* lazy and *extremely* dim-witted. Years of munching away on the lush, green grass in Finbar's Field, whilst failing to take exercise of any kind, had taken its toll on his physique to the extent that *waddling*, not galloping, was his preferred means of getting from A to B.

"Well," the horse spoke slowly as he carefully considered the question. "Usually, I find a patch of field to stand in and start eating the grass."

"Yes – go on..." Roger interrupted, his voice bubbling with excitement. "And what do you do then?"

"And when I've eaten all the grass in that particular patch of field, I wander over to a different bit."

"Yes, and then what?" the little frog beamed.

"And then I start eating that bit of grass. And once all the grass has been eaten in that particular patch..."

"Hang on a second," Roger cut in, aghast. "Let me get this straight - do you mean to tell me that you spend your days simply wandering hither and thither eating grass?"

"Yes." Norbert confirmed happily.

"And that's it?"

"Yes."

"I see."

There followed what is sometimes referred to as a 'pregnant' silence, broken only by the sound of Roger weeping gently.

Three times his hopes had been raised; *three* times they had been dashed to the ground. The life of the Daddy Longlegs, though pleasant enough while it lasted, had proven to be horrifyingly short. The mouse's daily routine, meanwhile, which saw it stalked relentlessly by a continual stream of would-be assassins, had proved if anything, to be a little *too* exciting for Roger's taste. But by far the most disturbing of all had been his encounter with Norbert. Never, in his worst nightmares had Roger ever considered the possibility that there could be a creature out there whose existence was even more boring than his own, and the discovery that this was indeed the case chilled him to the bone. *Could it be that this so-called Big Wide World was not all that it was cracked up to be?*

"Norbert?" the poor, deflated frog spoke quietly, all the enthusiasm having drained from his voice.

"Yes?" Norbert replied happily, having resumed his chomping for want of anything better to do.

"I've changed my mind; I do not wish to be a horse anymore."

And with these words, Roger turned and began his long, cheerless journey home.

Chapter 5

As midday approached, Father's enormous belly began to rumble. He was about to hop off his lily pad to check with Freda if his lunchtime flies were nearly ready when he perceived a gentle rustling among the bulrushes at the pond's edge.

"Roger!" he exclaimed, as his son crawled into view. "My dear boy – you're back!"

"Yes Father," Roger replied mournfully.

"Come, my dear fellow! You must sit beside me on your lily pad and tell me of Big Wide World. I'm assuming you've been on daring adventures, laughing death in the face and so forth?"

"No Father. I've only been gone an hour."

"Frank," a husky, familiar voice croaked from a neighbouring clump of bulrushes. "Is that you? What's all the noise about?"

"It's Roger, Dearest! Our long-lost son has returned from the Big Wide World!"

"Oh." Freda emerged and took her place at her husband's side. "Can we help you?" she sniffed, glaring at her son.

"I'm sorry for deserting you, Mother. I foolishly believed that the Big Wide World would be filled with wonder but I realize now that there's no place like home."

"Oh?"

"Yes Mother. I see now that my future is here with you and Father. Never again will I try to be what I am not. Never again will I venture beyond the perimeter of this pond. I swear to you both that I will never, ever attempt to go anywhere or do anything ever again."

"That's my boy!" Frank chuckled. "We always knew you would see sense in the end."

"Yes Father."

"Now then," Mother interrupted. "As you're back, you can make yourself useful and help me serve lunch."

"Yes Mother. What are we having today?"

"Flies."

"Yum," Roger whimpered, fighting back his nausea. "Shall I call Felicity and Florence to let them know it's ready?"

"No, Roger – that won't be necessary."

"Oh?"

"Yes, my dear boy," Father smiled. "Did we forget to mention that your sisters have gone away?"

"Gone away? But Father – I don't understand..."

"Yes Roger. At our insistence, Florence and Felicity have left home to study medicine at Cambridge."

"B... B... But..." the poor little frog reeled on his lily pad as the world began to spin around him.

"It's a difficult three-year course which will require a lot of hard work. Mind you – once they've graduated, they can both look forward to long, fulfilling careers in the medical profession."

"B... But..."

"Don't worry, my boy," the old frog chuckled. "As soon as lunch is finished I have a special treat planned for you this afternoon."

"Really Father?" the little frog gasped, a tiny spark of hope igniting in his heart.

"Yes, Roger. As *soon* as we have finished lunch, I thought we could park our bottoms, father and son, on our respective lily pads and then sit completely motionless, blinking our eyelids every once in a while until it grows dark."

In Roger's heart, the spark flickered and died.

"Come along Roger!" Mother growled heading off into the bulrushes. "These flies won't serve themselves, you know!"

Well, reader – are you still there? You are? Jolly good! Well - wasn't that the most miserable, depressing tale you've ever heard? I don't know about you, but it's completely ruined my day...

"But what, if anything, can we learn from Roger's tragic story?" I hear you cry. "Does it teach us that we should stick with what we know? That we should accept our lot in life without question, even if it falls short of our hopes and aspirations?"

I, for one, reader, do not think so. Because although his story is undeniably one of abject failure, it is important when we reflect upon it that we remember one all-important detail: Roger was a small, rather foolish frog, whereas you, reader, are not. With this vital difference in mind, we can conclude that we should ALL chase our dreams and NEVER accept second best. If you work hard enough and believe in yourself, you CAN be whatever you want to be in this life. Unless, of course, you happen to be a small, rather foolish frog named Roger...

The End

Ernie

Chapter 1

"Please Dad," the little girl cooed in her sweetest voice.

"No."

"Pleeeese!"

"No."

"Pleeeeese!"

"No."

"Pleeeeeese!"

"No."

"Pleeeeeeese!"

Dad had heard quite enough.

"Martha," he said sternly "do you *seriously* think I'm going to let that dog back in the house after what happened yesterday?"

Martha Miller chewed her lip thoughtfully as she ran her mind back over recent events.

"Oh – *that,*" she shrugged, remembering. "I'd forgotten all about *that*…" A day is a long time when you are nine years old…

"Well *I* certainly haven't," Dad snorted. "That dog is a pest and a menace to society, and as such, is banned from the house until further notice!"

"But Dad," Martha protested, tears welling in her eyes "Ernie didn't *mean* to poop in your slipper!"

Dad looked at her with amazement.

"Really?" he scoffed. "So let me get this straight - you are suggesting that this *mutt* of yours was simply strolling through the living room minding his own business when a poop shot unexpectedly out of his bottom and, by sheer chance, happened to land in my slipper?"

Martha gave her left pigtail a thoughtful twiddle. She had to admit it *did* seem a little far-fetched. *Perhaps she should tackle the thing from a different angle...*

"Well," she said, a note of reproach in her voice "it wasn't Ernie's fault - you should have checked in your slipper before you put it on..."

This had Dad rocketing from his armchair with outrage.

"Oh – I *see*," he exclaimed "now it all becomes clear - the whole thing was *my* fault! How *silly* of me not to realize..."

Sensing that she might have said the wrong thing, Martha maintained a respectful silence.

"Well – I've certainly learnt my lesson," Dad continued sarcastically. "Oh yes – in future, I shall take great care to check *each and every* item of footwear for unexpected dog dirt before I put it on!"

Martha studied him warily. Unless she was very much mistaken, Dad was beginning to lose his temper. His face was turning that funny bright purple sort of colour, which was always a sure sign...

"I'm sorry Dad," she sighed. "I didn't mean..."

"Well I'm afraid 'sorry' just isn't good enough, Martha. I have made my final decision on the matter."

"But..."

"As I live and breathe, Ernie does *not* set foot in this house until further notice!"

And with these bitter words, his face now a deep shade of crimson, Dad snatched up his newspaper and stormed out of the room, slamming the door behind him with a terrific *BANG!*

"Hmmf!" Martha shrugged to the empty living room. Persuading Dad to allow Ernie back into the family home had been a *bit* trickier than she had expected. Yet she was a very determined little girl and had never been one to give in without a fight. Dad may have won the opening skirmish, but the *real* battle was yet to come...

*

Out in the porch, tucked up warm and snug in his basket with his rubber bone, Ernie had listened in on the debate with much interest. Although he had welcomed Martha's stout defence of his actions, she had been mistaken in one key detail; he *had* quite deliberately pooped in Dad's slipper. Having been told time and time again that he must, under no circumstances, do his business on the rug, the sight of Dad's tartan size tens nestling behind the sofa had presented him with a perfect alternative. *How was he to know that the old man would make such a fuss?*

The discussion in the living room having concluded with Dad's dramatic exit, the little dog turned his attention back to his bone. Ernie simply *adored* his rubber bone; it was his most treasured possession in the whole wide world and he rarely ventured more than a few yards without it. Once upon a time it had been smooth, shiny and yellow; now it was brown, dirty and badly chewed up, but in spite of this, it had lost not an ounce of its charm as far as he was concerned.

"Ernie!"

A deafening yell from somewhere out in the hallway made him shrink back in his basket; *Martha*. Having come from a rescue centre as a puppy, Martha was the only real 'parent' Ernie had ever known, and he loved her almost (though not *quite*) as much as he loved his yellow rubber bone. If she had one fault, however, it was that her vocal chords operated at just two volumes, *LOUD* and ***VERY LOUD***. Still, her appearance on the scene usually meant one of two things; either there was some tasty food coming his way, or he was about to go out for a walk. Walks with Martha were always an adventure, with excitement and thrills guaranteed - quite unlike those he occasionally took with Mum or Dad, who simply dragged him along the same boring old route every day. Martha, on the other hand, liked to explore just as much as he did, and was more than happy to indulge him whenever he wanted to investigate the many fascinating objects and smells that he encountered among the pavements and hedgerows of the village.

Seconds later, the door of the porch opened and Martha strode in, Ernie rising to greet her with his usual ecstatic *woof*, his tail wagging frenziedly.

"Hiya," the little girl grinned, giving him a playful tickle behind the ear "shall we go out in the garden for a bit?"

Signalling his consent with a *yip* of glee, Ernie scampered back over to his basket to fetch his rubber bone before following her along the corridor and out through the back door, wagging his scruffy tail madly as he went.

*

At the sound of a rumble of thunder over the distant hills, Martha looked up at the sky with a worried frown.

"Looks like rain," she sighed. "Come on, Ernie - we'd better go back inside."

Ernie looked at her in stunned amazement. *Go back inside? Was she joking? No way was he going back inside! How could Martha, an apparently sensible girl, for whom he had always had the utmost respect, come out with such an utterly ridiculous suggestion? Did she not understand that a game as serious as 'Chuck the Bone' was not something that could be abandoned for the sake of a mere drop of rain?* It was thus with an air of mild reproach that he picked up his rubber bone, trotted back over to where she stood, and dropped it at her feet.

"Ok," the little girl shrugged, casting another anxious glance towards the heavens "but this will have to be the last throw..."

Woof! Ernie assented with a frantic wag of his tail. *He knew she would see sense...*

"Are you ready?" Martha grinned, waving the bone tantalisingly above her head. "As it's the last one, I'll make it the biggest throw ever!"

In later years, whenever he reflected on the episode that came to be known as *The Rubber Bone Tragedy,* Ernie would be forced to admit that getting his owner to throw his bone one last time had been a grave error. Martha, he should have known, was not the sort of girl who did things by halves, and if she promised the *biggest throw ever*, this was precisely what she would deliver. At first, as he watched his beloved toy whizzing through the air, it seemed to Ernie that all was well. True to her word, Martha had executed a fine, arcing throw that seemed destined to land smack bang in the middle of the compost heap at the bottom of the garden. Rummaging in the compost heap was one of Ernie's favourite pastimes, and the thought of retrieving his bone from such a splendid location filled him with excitement. *But wait... What was this? His bone wasn't going to land in the compost heap... No - it was sailing high above it... High above the compost heap... And into next door's garden!*

"Whoops!" Martha giggled as she turned to head inside. "Never mind – it was only an old bone anyway. Come on – let's get in quickly before it starts to rain."

Ernie, however, did not move. Instead, he merely sat, goggling in wide-eyed horror at the section of fence behind which his bone had just vanished. He did not notice the menacing growl of thunder above his head, nor did he heed the first heavy raindrops as they splashed on the end of his nose. *His bone was gone... His beloved bone to which no other bone could ever hope to compare had passed out of his life forever and ever!*

Or had it?

Chapter 2

"Come on, Ernie, eat up" Martha spoke with a tinge of anxiety as she pushed the food dish closer to the little dog's basket "they're *Bingo's Beefy Bites* – your favourite!"

Ernie frowned at the dish and gave it a disdainful sniff with his little black nose. The loss of his rubber bone had sent him into a state of mourning so deep that even *Bingo's Beefy Bites* had lost their appeal.

"Goodness me," the little girl sighed "you've hardly touched a thing for two days now! If this carries on, we'll have to take you to see Mr Pickles, the vet, and you know how much you hate going to see Mr Pickles."

Ernie considered this. In stating that he hated going to see Mr Pickles, Martha was quite correct; this was a man who prodded and poked at him, who made him swallow foul medicine, and who had even once had the downright nerve to stick a needle in his bottom! His owner was totally mistaken, however, if she believed that *any* threat, however dire, would induce him to eat so much as a morsel of food until his bone had been restored to its proper place at his side…

*

Ten minutes later, seated at the breakfast table, Martha addressed her parents through a moody mouthful of cornflakes.

"Guess what," she munched "Ernie wouldn't eat his breakfast again."

"Oh?" Dad, scanning his newspaper for last night's football results, showed very little interest in Ernie's eating habits.

"Yes – he's been like this ever since he lost his bone."

"Has he really?" Dad shrugged. "Well I'm sure he'll snap out of it sooner or later."

Martha, however, was not prepared to let the matter rest.

"Maybe we should go round and knock on Mrs Wiseman's door and ask her if we can have it back."

Reluctantly, Dad lowered his paper.

"No can do, I'm afraid," he said, shaking his head. "I thought we told you – Old Mrs Wiseman had to move out a few weeks ago.

She was getting very frail, so she's gone to live with her daughter."

The little girl frowned. This was genuinely disturbing news; Old Mrs Wiseman had been a nice lady who had, for many years, maintained an unwavering policy of dishing out toffees whenever hers and Martha's paths had crossed. *With Mrs Wiseman out of the picture, a new supplier of toffees would need to be sourced without delay...*

"Well, if the house is empty," she answered thoughtfully "perhaps we could just climb over the fence and get Ernie's bone."

"Oh no," Dad shook his head "it's not empty. Someone else has moved in – a guy by the name of Grimshaw."

"Well - perhaps you could ask him if we could have it back," Mum chipped in as she joined them at the table.

"Ask *him*?" Dad snorted, almost choking on his cornflakes. "Are you serious? Have you seen the guy? Why – he must be nearly seven feet tall..."

"But..."

"Shaved head, tattoos all over him, muscles like the Incredible Hulk...

"But…"

"No, Martha - if you think I'm going to knock on that monster's door and ask if he fancies joining me for a game of *hunt the rubber bone* in his back garden, I am afraid you are very much mistaken!"

Mum turned to her husband with a hint of reproach.

"Of course, if you're scared of him…"

"Oh no," Dad lied, his cheeks pinkening slightly "don't be silly, Claire. Of *course* I'm not scared. I just don't want to… to *disturb* him, that's all. I'm sure he's a very busy man."

Mum was about to reply, however when she looked up, she saw only an empty space at the table where her husband had been. The slam of a car door in the driveway, quickly followed by the revving of an engine confirmed that he had fled the scene and was on his way to work.

"I have an idea," she said, turning her attention back to Martha who was toying at her cornflakes with the same apathy as that which Ernie had displayed towards his *Beefy Bites*. "How about I give you some pocket money and you can call at the pet shop on the way home from school and buy him a new one?"

Martha twiddled her spoon thoughtfully at the suggestion. While Mum's scheme certainly had its merits, it suffered from one fatal flaw; Ernie, she suspected, would only be satisfied by the restoration of *his* rubber bone. Any replica, be it the shiniest, most expensive rubber bone in the universe, simply wouldn't do and would be treated as a rank impostor. *Still s*he told herself *in a crisis as serious as this, anything was worth a try...*

"Ok Mum," she sighed, hopping down from her seat "I expect five pounds should be enough."

"*Five pounds?*" Mum gasped, fumbling in her purse. "That seems like an awful lot of money for a rubber bone, Martha. Are you *sure* they cost that much?"

"Positive," the little girl grinned, snatching the note "*everything* costs a fortune these days. At least that's what Dad always says..."

*

As lunchtime approached, with Mum and Dad at work, and Martha at school, Ernie trotted down the garden path, his scruffy features set in a look of fierce and steely determination. Earlier that morning, he had conducted a thorough survey of the fence that separated his own garden from that of the next door neighbour, and in doing so had discovered a loose plank down at the far bottom corner, behind the compost heap. It must, he concluded, have come loose during the winter storms, and would provide a perfect opening through which a dog of his slight stature could comfortably pass. The garden on the other side of the fence represented mysterious and uncharted territory to Ernie, and the thought of the dangers that might await him there filled him with a nameless dread. And yet he knew that he had little choice; *if he ever wanted to see his beloved rubber bone again, he would have to brave the unknown, whatever the risks may be.* His mind made up, he crept forward and nudged the loose plank to one side with his little wet nose.

"I wouldn't go in there if I were you."

The sound of a shrill voice piping up behind him startled the little dog, sending him rocketing skyward in terror. Spinning on his heels, Ernie was astonished to discover that he was being addressed by a small, somewhat mangy-looking mouse from its perch upon a rusty old wheelbarrow.

"I b… beg your pardon?" he quavered.

"Allow me to introduce myself," said the mouse. "Montgomery's the name. I merely remarked that I would strongly advise against your going through that hole in the fence."

Ernie peered at the dark opening with growing alarm.

"Oh?" he trembled, turning his attention back to the tiny creature. "But my rubber bone's in there, you see, and I just thought I'd pop in and get it back…"

"A rubber bone, eh?" Montgomery shook his head. "I'm really not sure it's worth risking certain death for the sake of a rubber bone."

A cold chill coursed down Ernie's spine.

"C… Certain death?" he croaked. "W… What do you mean by that?"

"Oh yes," the mouse continued. "If you crawl through that hole, I very much doubt you'd survive for more than a few minutes."

"Allow me to introduce myself," said the mouse. "Montgomery's the name."

This was definitely not the kind of thing that Ernie wanted to hear.

"B… But why?" he gulped. "Surely there can't be anything *that* bad in there."

"Oh, but I'm afraid there is," Montgomery squeaked from his perch upon the wheelbarrow. "There's a dog. Or, to be more precise, a *big* bulldog."

Again, this was bad news for Ernie. As a *small* dog, he had always been rather afraid of big dogs. They were just so… *BIG!* For a few seconds, he fell into a gloomy silence as he considered the position of affairs. Then a thought occurred to him.

"Just because he's big, it doesn't mean he won't be nice," he said, his furry face brightening. "Sometimes big dogs are the friendliest of all."

"Oh no," the mouse shook its head again, dashing his hopes in an instant "not this one."

"Oh?"

"No, my friend – I'm afraid he's not in the *least* bit friendly."

"Oh dear!" Ernie quivered.

"Indeed," Montgomery continued "it's fair to say that he's a nasty piece of work - one of those vicious, snarling blighters, all slavering jaws and gnashing teeth – you know the sort. As a matter of fact, *he's* the reason I've had to move house."

"Really?" Ernie quivered some more.

"Oh yes," said the mouse. "I *used* to have a lovely cosy place under Old Mrs Wiseman's shed, but thanks to him I've been forced to find alternative accommodation underneath this wheelbarrow."

The little dog's eyes widened with worry. "Why?" he gulped. "What happened?"

"Oh nothing much," Montgomery sighed. "He spotted me in the garden the other day and just happened to mention during the course of our conversation that if he ever set eyes on me again, he would chew me up into a sort of fine mincemeat before swallowing me in a single gulp."

"Yikes!"

"Yes," the mouse nodded in agreement. "Downright unfriendly, if you ask me."

A nervous silence ensued as Ernie's vivid imagination conjured up images of the terrible beast that lurked on the other side of the fence. But then a further image popped into his head, one which banished all of his fears in an instant; he pictured that very same terrible beast chewing on *his* rubber bone! Big dog or no big dog, this was simply unacceptable; the bone *had* to be retrieved at all costs. *What was the point of having a future anyway, if the future in question did not contain yellow rubber bones?* And so, with his steely courage flooding back in spades, Ernie puffed out his little chest defiantly and turned once again to the mouse.

"Thank you for your warning," he said "but I fear I must go. If I do not return, at least I will have perished in the noblest of causes. Goodbye, my friend – perhaps we shall meet again some sunny day…" And with these brave words, he scampered over to the hole in the fence and disappeared through it.

"Very well," a squeaky voice called after him "but don't say I didn't warn you!"

Chapter 3

"Pink's no good." Martha stood at the counter of the pet shop, scowling ferociously at Mr Longbottom, the owner. "It's got to be yellow."

"I'm very sorry," the portly bald-headed man replied, struggling to keep his cool "but as I have already explained, we've sold out of yellow bones and our next delivery isn't due until Friday."

"*Friday?*" the little girl gasped in horror. "That's *ages* away!"

"It's the day after tomorrow."

"But I've already *told* you," Martha pleaded, turning the ferocity of her scowl up a notch "Ernie's gone off his food 'cos he's lost his yellow bone!"

The shopkeeper, who had been having a bad day even before this little pipsqueak entered his life, had heard quite enough.

"Now listen here, Miss…" he said through gritted teeth.

"Miller – Martha Miller," came the spirited reply.

"Well, Miss Miller - I have clearly explained the situation regarding our stock of yellow rubber bones..."

"Yes but..."

"If you find this to be unacceptable, then I would politely suggest that you take your custom elsewhere..."

"Yes but..."

"However, if you wish to *try* your dog with a pink bone, I am prepared, given the circumstances, to offer you a small discount."

The mention of a discount caught Martha's interest.

"Oh?" she said, her eyes narrowing. "How much?"

"They usually cost three pounds, but you can have it for two."

Martha gave her left pigtail a thoughtful twiddle as she considered the offer.

"I've only got a pound," she replied finally "and I still think even *that's* too much for that rotten old pink thing."

Growing ever more flustered, Mr Longbottom gaped at the little girl, searching her steely blue eyes for any sign of weakness but finding only stout defiance. He was a beaten man and he knew it...

“Here,” he groaned, pressing the bone into an outstretched grubby hand “you can have it for free – just please leave me alone!”

“Hmm, I’ll *try* it, I s’pose,” said Martha “but if Ernie doesn’t like it, you can bet I’ll be back here first thing on Friday…”

“Very well,” the poor man gibbered “whatever you say.”

“Provided he hasn’t *starved* to death in the meantime, that is,” Martha added darkly as she turned to march out of the shop “and *then* you’ll be sorry…”

As the door slammed with a terrific *BANG!* Mr Longbottom mopped his shiny forehead with a mixture of relief and dismay. *When he had decided to pursue a career as a shopkeeper, he had never expected his life to be quite as stressful as this…*

*

His heart beating like a hammer, Ernie crept as quietly as he could through the thick undergrowth. In recent years, Old Mrs Wiseman had been too frail to look after her garden properly, and as a result the grass was waist-high and the paths and paving stones barely visible beneath a dense tangle of weeds and brambles. To a dog of Ernie's modest proportions it was not unlike the jungles of the Darkest Congo; *how on earth would he ever find his beloved bone in a place like this?*

*

"Tumty tumty tum," Martha sang boisterously to herself as she skipped up the steps and through the front door, flinging her school bag down in the porch.

"Mum," she hollered "I'm home!"

"Yes dear," Mum sighed, appearing at the kitchen door. "I thought I heard you come in. Did you have a nice day at school?"

"Not really," came the honest reply "it was dead boring. Where's Ernie?"

"I think he's out in the back garden, dear. Please don't march through the hallway in those muddy shoes.

"I stopped at Longbottom's and got him a new bone," Martha bellowed, marching through the hallway in her muddy shoes.

"Ooh," Mum smiled "that's good."

"Except it's a pink one," the little girl roared as she opened the door that led to the back garden "and I'm not sure if Ernie likes pink."

"Well dear, you never know. Perhaps he'll…"

BANG! went the back door as Martha marched out into the garden in search of her pet.

*

Ernie had not travelled far through the undergrowth when he became aware of a curious sound up ahead. He froze, listening intently, one ear cocked; *snoring.* Intrigued, he sat up on his hind legs and sniffed the air. *What was that? Could it be true? Yes - it was but the faintest of whiffs, yet there was no mistaking it… Ernie had picked up the scent of his bone!* With a *yip* of delight, the little dog bounded forward, his heart filled with joy at the prospect of being reunited with the love of his life. Indeed, his excitement was such that he forgot all about his conversation with Montgomery, and it was only when he emerged from the undergrowth that the mouse's dire warnings came back to him. Directly ahead, there was a stone patio, in the corner of which there stood a large dog's kennel. Worse still, judging by the snoring coming from within its walls, this particular large dog's kennel was clearly home to a very large dog.

Silently, stealthily, Ernie crept forward to investigate. Sure enough, sprawled fast asleep, with just its head and front paws protruding from the kennel, he discerned what was, without any shadow of a doubt, the biggest bulldog he had ever seen. And nestled snugly between those paws, those terrible, bear-like front paws, lay his beloved bone! Hardly daring to breathe, Ernie crouched, still as a statue, as he considered his next move. As he saw it, there were two factors which might work in his favour:

Factor 1: The beast was, at least for now, fast asleep.

Factor 2: His bone was nestled *between* its paws, not *underneath* them. *If he was very, very quiet and very, very careful, Ernie felt sure he could extract it without disturbing the slumbering brute.*

And so, still holding his breath, he stole forward until he was close enough to read the brass name tag on the collar that hung around the monster's neck. *Max* it said. *Now was the moment of reckoning*; slowly, delicately, he reached out a front paw…

"Ernie!" a familiar voice bellowed from somewhere back in his own garden.

The little dog paused. *Drat! It was Martha, back from school already...*

"ERNIE!" the voice sounded again, even louder this time.

Max stirred and let out a great yawn, revealing a fearsome set of fangs; fortunately, his eyes, for the time being, remained tightly shut. In sheer desperation, Ernie grasped at his bone with a quivering paw and gave it a gentle tug. *A split second longer and he would have it! If only Martha would keep quiet...*

"EEEEERRRRNIEEE!" came the ear-splitting roar from the other side of the garden fence.

Frozen to the spot, his outstretched paw still resting on his beloved bone, Ernie could only goggle in silent horror as Max let out another tremendous yawn before slowly opening one sleepy, bloodshot eye…

Chapter 4

Through the course of his short life, Ernie had found himself in many an awkward situation. The time when he had chewed Dad's brand new *Nike* trainers to a pulp was one that sprang to mind. *How was he to know they'd cost a hundred and fifty pounds?* Then there was the occasion when he had inadvertently peed on Mum's laptop. *Again, hardly his fault - if they went leaving things lying around on the living room floor, what did they expect him to do?* On both occasions, he had been caught red handed (or red-*pawed*, to be more precise) and been punished accordingly. Neither of the above, however, was anywhere near as awkward as his current predicament. There is, you see, a firm code of conduct among dogs under which it is strictly forbidden under *any* circumstances to steal the bone of a fellow canine. It is seen as dastardly and taboo – an abominable crime that only the vilest of villains would ever *dream* of committing. *'Yes,'* you cry *'but Ernie wasn't actually stealing the bone - he was only trying to get one back that already belonged to him.'* Yes, reader – but, whilst this is undoubtedly true, the problem was that Max clearly was not aware of this fact. As far as *he* was concerned, the yellow rubber bone that he had found in his back garden earlier that day was his and his alone, and he therefore took great exception to the sight of this sneaky little thief attempting to steal it from him.

Hastily withdrawing his paw, Ernie knew he would have to think, and think quickly.

"Oh - hello there neighbour," he gurgled. "Lovely day, isn't it?"

"Grrrrrr!"

"I… I must say, it's very nice to meet you. My name's Ernie – I live at the Miller's house next door."

"Grrrrrrrr!"

Somewhat rattled, the little dog retreated a few steps and studied his adversary. This 'Max' seemed to have a very limited vocabulary, and it was clearly not going to be easy to strike up anything resembling a civilized conversation. *Perhaps he ought to try a more direct approach…*

"I'm terribly sorry if I've disturbed you," he said in a polite, yet firm, voice "but I was wondering if you might be kind enough to let me have my bone back."

This drew an immediate response from Max, though it was not the kind that Ernie had hoped for.

"My bone!" he growled, slapping a huge paw down on the rubber toy as if to underline his point.

Hmmm Ernie thought to himself. *This is going to be even trickier than I thought...*

"Ah yes," he nodded gravely. "I quite understand why you might *think* it belongs to you, but it's actually one of mine that just happened to be thrown into your garden by accident. My owner, Martha, you see..."

"My bone!" the massive dog repeated, rising menacingly up onto its haunches.

Ernie sighed. He had hoped to retrieve his property through peaceful diplomacy, yet it was becoming increasingly obvious that this was not to be. And so, with the air of a grownup addressing a naughty child, he puffed out his little chest and addressed the bulldog in his sternest voice.

"Now look here," he woofed "I don't want any trouble, but I demand that you give me my bone back right this minute!"

Max looked at him with a puzzled expression which quickly changed to one of amusement.

“Or what?” he growled with a smirk.

A simple enough question, you might think, yet it was one which had Ernie completely baffled. *If this monstrous brute flatly refused to give him his bone, what, in actual fact, could he do about it?*

“Or… Or else,” hc gulped “y… you shall have to face the consequences!”

Max frowned. Though he did not understand what *consequences* were, he *was* intelligent enough to realize that he was being threatened. And not only was he being threatened, but he was being threatened by a jumped-up little pipsqueak less than half his size. After a brief moment of consideration, he responded as any self-respecting bulldog would; with a blood-curdling roar, he coiled his muscles and made a sudden spring at his tormentor. Frozen to the spot with sheer terror, Ernie could only shut his eyes tightly as he awaited his ghastly fate. *Could anyone save him now?*

*

At that precise moment another roar of a similar volume could be heard in the hallway of the Miller household.

"MUM!" Martha bellowed up the stairs.

No response.

"MUUUUUUM!" she repeated, twice as loudly as before.

On the upstairs landing, a door flew open and Mum came hurtling down the stairs, almost breaking her neck in the process.

"Martha!" she cried, crouching to examine her daughter. "What's wrong? Are you hurt?"

Martha gave her a quizzical look.

"'Course I'm not *hurt*," she shrugged. "What makes you think I'm hurt?"

"Then why were you screaming up the stairs like that?" Mum gasped.

"I wasn't *screaming*," came the simple reply. "I was just *calling* to ask if you'd seen Ernie."

"Ernie?" Mum shook her head in bewilderment. "I was upstairs on the telephone to your Uncle Brian. Why would I have seen Ernie?"

"I just thought you might have, that's all," Martha scowled.

"Well I haven't," sighed Mum. "Now if you don't mind, I'll call your uncle back and let him know everything's ok. He must be wondering what on earth is going on."

But Martha wasn't finished yet.

"Never mind calling Uncle Brian - p'raps you should call the police instead."

Mum paused halfway up the stairs.

"The police?" she frowned. "Why on earth would I want to call the police?"

"Well - what if Ernie's been kidnapped?" Martha replied earnestly.

"Kidnapped?" Mum was growing more bewildered by the second. "Martha – no self-respecting kidnapper would want to steal a dog like Ernie…"

"Oh?" the little girl retorted, offended. "Why wouldn't they? Ernie's a very nice dog, I'll have you know, and…"

"Yes, but he's not an expensive pedigree, is he?" Mum interrupted, continuing on her way up the stairs. "Anyway – I'm sure he'll probably just be snuffling about down in the compost heap like he usually is."

"He isn't. I've checked."

"Well I'm sure he'll turn up sooner or later. Now, for goodness' sake – go outside and get some fresh air!"

Chapter 5

Long ago, when he was but a mere pup, Ernie's mother had told him about something called *divine intervention*. It was, she explained, a kind of unseen, magical force that had a habit of saving the day at the very moment when it seems like all hope is lost. As he crouched, fully expecting to feel the bite of the huge dog's teeth upon his person, Ernie was surprised to hear only a strangled 'yelp!' *Could it be that the good old hand of divine intervention had stepped in to rescue him in his hour of need?* Blinking open one frightened eye, he quickly saw that it had done nothing of the sort; Max, he now realized, had been tied to his kennel with a stout metal chain all along, and it was this chain, rather than any divine intervention, that had yanked him backwards, mid-leap, and deposited him in an ungainly heap on the concrete patio. Observing his stricken foe, Ernie briefly wondered whether it might be worth a stab at reopening negotiations about his bone, however the sight of Max beginning to stir quickly made him abandon the idea; the chain, though fairly sturdy, was a decidedly old and rusty-looking affair which could not be relied on to restrain the brute forever. No – just as Martha had done in her earlier battle with Dad, he would beat a tactical retreat and resume hostilities at a later point when the odds were more in his favour. And so, with a light *yip* of defiance, the little dog turned tail and scampered hurriedly away through the undergrowth.

*

"There you are!" Martha grinned as she spotted the small, furry figure trotting up the path. But as Ernie drew nearer, her grin quickly turned to a frown of dismay. "Goodness me," she gasped "look at the state of you! What on *earth* have you been doing?"

Ernie gave her a blank look. Perhaps his ordeal with Max had left him looking a tad scruffier than normal, but he had far more important things than appearances on his mind at the moment.

"Woof," he replied with a somewhat half-hearted wag of his tail.

"Never mind," said Martha, giving him an affectionate tickle under the chin. "Come along with me – I've a special surprise waiting for you."

Moments later, the little dog found himself being ushered into the porch where, nestling in his basket, he noted a mysterious object, carefully wrapped in gift paper. Though he could not guess what it could be, there was something about its size and shape that seemed oddly familiar. Approaching it warily, Ernie gave it an exploratory sniff with his little black nose.

Mmmm he thought to himself. *I'm sure that reminds me of something...*

Then it came to him; *it was the scent of rubber or, to be more precise, the scent of a rubber bone! Somehow, impossible though it seemed, Martha had magically retrieved his beloved bone and put it back in his basket where it belonged!*

His heart racing, Ernie goggled at her in awe.

"Well," Martha laughed, "aren't you going to open it up and see what it is?"

Ernie needed no further encouragement. With a *yip* of unbridled glee, he seized the paper package in his teeth and tore into it like a dog possessed.

*

Through in the kitchen, Dad had arrived home from work and was busy making himself a restorative cup of tea when Mum entered the room.

"Hiya," she said brightly. "How's your day been?"

"Alright, I suppose," Dad huffed. He had recently acquired a new manager in the office, a fellow by the name of Simpkin, whom he disliked intensely, but whose company he was forced to endure for eight hours a day; for this reason, Dad was rarely in the best of moods by the time he got home from work. "How about you?"

"Not too bad," Mum sat down at the table opposite him. "Martha seems in a funny mood, though – even grumpier than usual!"

At this, Dad shuddered visibly, almost choking on his tea.

"Grumpier than usual?" he spluttered. "But surely that's impossible!"

Mum took a deep breath. She knew that what she was about to say wouldn't please her husband, but she was determined to voice it anyway.

"I've been thinking," she spoke in her breeziest voice "that perhaps we're being a bit hard on her."

"Hard on her?" Dad gave her a puzzled look. "What do you mean, *hard on her*?"

"Well – I mean this business of banning Ernie from the house. Martha hasn't actually done anything wrong and she likes having him on her knee when she's watching TV in the evenings."

As expected, her remark went down like a lead balloon.

"Really Claire!" Dad snapped, rising from his chair. "I thought we were both agreed he'd have to stay in the porch."

"Yes but…"

"After what he did to my slipper…"

"Yes George, but it was only an accident…"

Dad, however, was in no mood to listen.

"Sometimes I wonder what the world's coming to," he huffed, shaking his head in dismay. "Everyone you meet these days seems to be obsessed with dogs. Anywhere you try and go – any street, any park, any beach, there are dogs, dogs, pesky dogs as far as the eye can see!"

Mum was already wishing she had never raised the subject.

"Look," she sighed "let's just forget about it for now – we'll talk about it some other time."

But she was too late – Dad was already working up a full head of steam.

"Well," he snorted "don't mind me. You go ahead and fill the whole house with dogs if you like!"

"Really George – there's no need to be like that…"

"How about bringing in a few dozen cats as well, just for good measure."

"Now you're being stupid."

"Ha!" Dad scoffed. "Me? Being stupid? For objecting to having my slippers filled with dog dirt?"

"Look George - I didn't mean…"

But Dad was already heading for the door.

"Well – I'll leave it up to you. In the meantime, I'm off to the *one* place in the whole wide world where I know for certain that I won't be plagued by pesky animals!"

And with these bitter words, he stomped from the room, pausing only to express his sincere hope that his wife wouldn't be bitten to death by fleas.

Stifling a scream of frustration, Mum watched him go; *if this carried on much longer, she'd end up in bed again with one of her migraines...*

Dad's intended destination was the garden shed. A good thirty yards from the house, it had often come in useful as a place of refuge, offering sanctuary and solitude whenever the outside world and all its worries got too much. The outside world and all its worries had been getting too much quite regularly of late, and for this reason, he had installed a comfy chair in which he planned to sit and while away an hour or so with a relaxing book. Half way down the garden path, crouched behind a large rhododendron bush, he encountered his daughter, Martha. She appeared, he noted, to be messing with the new garden hosepipe he had bought only last week – the very same hosepipe which she had been banned from touching under pain of death.

"Oh - hiya, Dad," she said, startled. She hadn't realized he was back from work just yet.

"What do you think you are doing?" Dad spoke tersely.

"Oh nothin' much," Martha shrugged. "I was a bit bored, so I jus' thought I'd help you and Mum by waterin' the garden."

This had Dad's blood pressure rocketing again.

"Oh you did, did you?" he barked. "I take it you've forgotten what happened the last time you 'helped' to water the garden?"

"Yes but…"

"The whole place was flooded. It was like something out of the Old Testament - all of my lettuces were completely drowned!"

"Yes Dad, but that was last week…"

"Look, Martha – I've had a very stressful day at work and don't need any more arguments right now. Why don't you go and do something useful, like finishing your homework, perhaps?"

And with this, in Martha's opinion, *outrageous* suggestion, he continued on his way to the sanctuary of his beloved shed. He had barely travelled a few paces, however, when a booming voice came from behind him.

"Guess what, Dad?" it bellowed. "I bought Ernie a new bone from Longbottom's today. I just gave it to him, but I'm not sure if he liked it."

"Oh?" Dad frowned. "Why ever not? Surely one rubber bone is the same as another."

"Not really," came the earnest reply. "It's pink, you see, and I don't think Ernie likes pink."

Chapter 6

In stating that she wasn't sure whether Ernie *liked* his new rubber bone, Martha had failed to grasp the true depths of the little dog's feelings towards it. Ernie didn't just *dislike* his new toy – he *hated* it more than he had ever hated anything in his whole life. As the contents of the package had revealed themselves, the state of wild excitement in which he had torn off the wrapping paper had quickly changed to one of stunned horror. *How could Martha do this to him? How could she be so cruel? Deliberately raising his hopes by putting a parcel the exact size and shape of his beloved bone in his basket, knowing full well that it contained this horrid pink imposter?*

With a *yip* of disgust, Ernie had turned on his heels and headed straight for the door, determined to put as much distance as possible between himself and the ghastly object. It was as he was tottering past the compost heap a few minutes later, still in a state of deep shock, that he was hailed by a familiar squeaky voice.

"You didn't manage to get it back then?"

"Sorry?" Ernie blinked at the mangy little mouse who was once again addressing him from its perch on the upturned wheelbarrow.

"Your bone." Montgomery trilled. "I'm assuming you didn't manage to get it back from that blighter next door."

"No," the little dog sighed. "He's got it in his kennel and thinks that it's his. There's no way I'll ever see that again..."

"Nonsense."

Ernie's heart rate quickened.

"W...What do you mean?" he stammered. *Was there still, even now, a chance he would get his beloved bone back?*

Montgomery hopped down from his wheelbarrow and scampered over to where the little dog stood, looking him squarely in the eye.

"I simply pointed out that your statement that you would never see your bone again was, in my opinion, nonsense."

"But..."

"I could just as easily have described it as *drivel, twaddle* or *poppycock...*"

"But Montgomery," Ernie protested "you told me yourself how scary Max was. I'm only small – how could I ever stand a chance against him?"

"Dear me," the little mouse scoffed "if everyone took that attitude, nobody would ever achieve anything. You know what King Robert the Bruce of Scotland told his troops shortly before they thrashed the English at the battle of Bannockburn, don't you?"

"No," Ernie replied truthfully.

"He said 'if at first you don't succeed, try, try and try again', and that is precisely what *we* must do."

Ernie fell silent for a moment whilst he considered this.

"That's all very well," he said, shaking his scruffy head doubtfully "but what about those teeth? And those claws?"

"Yes, yes, yes," Montgomery snorted with a dismissive wave of his tiny paw "he may indeed possess teeth and claws, but what he doesn't have is *brains!*"

Ernie's heart rate quickened further as sensed a glimmer of hope.

"What we must do," the mouse continued, warming to his theme "is come up with a cunning plan."

"Yes but..."

"It's quite simple. All we have to do is find a way to lure the beast from its lair..."

Ernie frowned as he pondered the mouse's words.

"Are you saying we should try to tempt Max away from his kennel?"

"Precisely," Mongomery grinned. "And with Max out of the picture, your bone will be there for the taking! Now listen carefully – here's what we'll do..."

*

In the shed, relaxing in the blissful comfort of his armchair, Dad let out a long, contented yawn as he finished the chapter of the detective novel he had been reading. Though he had almost reached the bit where the identity of the murderer was about to be revealed, the warm sun blazing through the shed windows had made him drowsy, so much so that he felt unable to continue without first having taken a restorative nap. At least he was guaranteed peace and quiet here in his dog-free place of refuge, and besides, he could always find out who the killer was when he woke up. And so, placing the book down on the shelf beside him, he closed his eyes and was fast asleep in a matter of moments.

*

Ernie crept cautiously into the porch where his bowl of Bingo's Beefy Bites lay, still untouched, from breakfast time. Had Martha been present, she would have been deeply relieved to witness him apparently tucking into his food with great gusto; what she would not have known, however, was that Ernie had not the slightest intention of *swallowing* the meaty snacks – instead, he was merely squeezing as many into his mouth as possible in order to transport them to a secret, unknown destination. His cheeks bulging, he trotted back out into the garden and off down the path, only to return a few minutes later in order to repeat the same action. A further two trips and the bowl was empty.

Down at the compost heap, Montgomery surveyed the little mound of food in the same critical way that a general might survey his stocks of ammunition.

"Hmmm," he pondered. "There's not *quite* as many Beefy Bites as I had anticipated, but hopefully there will be enough to get the job done."

"So what do we do now?" Ernie said, glancing dubiously at the soggy chunks of meat.

"You'd better leave this next part to me," the mouse replied. "Stealth is critical on a mission such as this, and my tiny size should enable me to move back and forth through enemy territory undetected."

"Yes but…"

"You, in the meantime, must adopt a defensive position behind that dustbin over there and await my signal."

Ernie was growing more confused by the minute.

"Signal?" he frowned. "What sort of signal?"

Montgomery scratched his tiny chin.

"Yes," he whispered. "That's a good point. It needs to be something subtle – something that will not arouse the suspicions of the enemy."

For a few seconds, he fell into a pensive silence.

"I've got it!" he exclaimed, jumping up with excitement. "I shall make a sound like the hoot of an owl."

"The hoot of an owl?" Ernie shook his head. "But that's ridiculous - it's the middle of the afternoon."

"Never mind that – it's what Special Forces always do in these situations. As soon as you hear the hooting sound, you'll know that the coast is clear and that it's time for you to move."

"Ok, but what if…"

"Shhh, my friend," Montgomery hissed "now listen carefully – here's what I need you to do when you hear the signal."

There followed a great deal of whispering as the mouse explained to Ernie in great detail what his role in the operation would be.

"Well?" he whispered, having concluded his piece. "Is that clear?"

"Yes," the little dog gulped. "At least, I think it is..."

"Very good," said the mouse. "Then I'll be off. If I do not return, please do your best to ensure that I have an honourable burial, and don't forget to inform my next of kin."

And before Ernie could reply, he hurriedly scooped a Bingo's Beefy Bite underneath each of his tiny armpits and vanished through the gap in the fence into next door's garden.

Chapter 7

Max awoke with a deep yawn. Having recovered from his encounter with the peculiar little dog from next door, he had soon drifted off into a pleasant slumber in the summer sunshine. Opening his eyes, he glanced sleepily around at his surroundings; *yes – his new rubber bone was still there – heaven help anyone who dared to try and pinch it again!* Satisfied that all was well, he rose to a sitting position and wiped a slobber of drool that was dripping from his chin with one massive paw. Max was a classic example of what is sometimes referred to as a *slobbery dog*, and he often awoke to find a pool of warm dribble in the area where he had been resting his head. Then he spotted something unusual; barely a yard from where he had been sleeping, there was what appeared to be a small chunk of meat. Rising stiffly on his haunches, he waddled forward to investigate. A quick sniff at the mysterious morsel was all that was required for a positive identification; *why – unless he was very much mistaken, it was a Bingo's Beefy Bite! He hadn't tasted one of those in ages!* Without further ado, he shot out his long, slobbery tongue and gobbled it up. Puzzled, but nevertheless pleasantly surprised by this unexpected treat, Max was turning to head back to his kennel when he spotted *another* one a few yards further down the path. Drooling as he had never drooled before, he took an eager step towards it, only to be reminded by the rattling of his chain that he was still attached to his kennel.

"Drat!" he muttered to himself. *"There's no way it'll stretch that far..."*

And yet when he turned around to look at the chain, Max was astonished to discover that it had been unfastened by a mysterious, unseen hand. An intelligent dog might, at this point, have sensed that there was something fishy going on, however, as we have already established, Max was *not* an intelligent dog. Far from it; he was a nincompoop of the first order. And so, with a greedy *woof* of delight, he trotted gamely off down the path and gobbled up the second chunk of meat in a single gulp. It tasted *even* more delicious than the first one! *But wait - what was this? Unless he was very much mistaken, there appeared to be a THIRD*

Beefy Bite a little further ahead down the path! Today wasn't turning out to be so bad after all...

*

Hunkered down in his hidey-hole behind the dustbin, Ernie was growing more nervous with every passing moment. It seemed to him that Montgomery had been gone for hours and hours (though it was, in fact, somewhere in the region of four and a half minutes). *Where was he? Had Max got hold of him and chewed him into a fine mincemeat, just as he had promised?* Then he heard it – the sound of a large creature advancing through the undergrowth nearby. Peeping out from behind his dustbin, Ernie was astonished to see Max's bulky form advancing up the path towards him. *He must have forced his way through the gap in the fence! Was this all part of Montgomery's plan? If so, the mouse certainly hadn't told him about it...* Hardly daring to breathe, the little dog watched, keeping deathly still as the monster passed within inches of his hiding place, still hot on the trail of Bingo's

Beefy Bites that led away up the path through the Miller's garden.

Barely had Max vanished from sight when Ernie was alerted by another sound. Cocking his right ear, he listened carefully… *Yes – there it went again – a sound that had a curious resemblance to the hoot of an owl; Montgomery's signal – it was time to act!* Plucking up all of the courage he could muster, the little dog crept from his hideout and scurried through the gap in the fence into next door's garden. But even as he began to make his way through the undergrowth towards Max's kennel, Ernie spotted a fatal flaw in the mouse's plan; *as soon as the trail of Beefy Bites ran out, Max would surely turn and head for home, and when he did, there was a distinct danger that they might bump into one another. It would not, Ernie feared, be a happy reunion, especially if he happened to be carrying the bone he had just pinched from the bulldog's kennel…*

"Montgomery, you nitwit," he cursed under his breath. "If only you'd thought of a way of keeping him busy for longer!"

Little did he know that the cunning little mouse had already seen to it that Max would be kept out of the picture for as long as was deemed necessary…

*

In the shed, Dad was dreaming deeply. It was a pleasant dream, one he had on a regular basis about a world in which there were no dogs – not a single one. Why this was, he did not know, nor did he care. All that mattered was that in this canine-free paradise, he was able to walk the streets and enjoy the scenery without having to keep his eyes constantly trained on the pavement for fear of stepping in something unpleasant. Equally, in this heavenly place, he was able to put on his slippers each morning with the carefree certainty that there would not be anything squidgy inside them. *But wait – what was that? A curious noise – a strange, growling sort of noise, just the kind of sound a dog would make.* In his sleep, Dad twitched restlessly as the contented smile faded from his face.

"Grrrrrr!"

There it was again! But that was impossible – there WERE no dogs in this wondrous dreamland…

"Grrrrrrrr!"

With a violent start, Dad sat bolt upright and opened his eyes. He blinked. And he blinked again. And again. *No – this could not be. He must be having a nightmare – yes that was it... He was still dreaming. There couldn't possibly be a large, ferocious-looking bulldog sitting in the shed with him... Could there?*

*

His heart beating double time, Ernie advanced warily up the path towards Max's kennel. As it came into view, he was relieved to see that all seemed quiet; *Montgomery's plan to lure the beast away had clearly worked.* And yet the closer he got, the more his spirits sank, for of his bone, his beloved, treasured bone, there was simply no sign. Unsure how to proceed, the little dog hesitated. *Should he abort the mission and settle for a new life with the Pink Imposter? Was it possible that, given the healing hands of time, he could learn to love it in the same way he had loved his old bone?* Ernie very much doubted it. *Still, it appeared that he had little choice. He had done his best – he was only sorry that his best had not been good enough...*

And so, with a sad sigh of resignation, he turned to head for home. Yet barely had he trotted a few paces, when something miraculous happened. It was, as we have previously mentioned, a still and sunny day, yet out of nowhere, a sudden gust of wind blew up, filling the little dog's senses with something all too familiar, a wonderful, delectable fragrance that almost made his heart burst with joy... *HIS BONE! Yet again, Ernie had picked up the scent of his bone!*

Spinning on his heels, he rushed back towards the kennel and dived in. Sniffling and snuffling like an undersized bloodhound, he followed the sweet scent further and further in until his little black nose came into contact with the back wall, and there, right in the darkest corner, hidden underneath a scruffy old blanket, he discerned a familiar knobbly shape. With a *yip* of glee, he seized the blanket in his teeth and hurled it to one side...

Chapter 8

Very, very slowly, his heart skipping to a salsa beat, Dad rose from his chair.

"S… Steady boy," he bleated. "Th…There's a good boy – nice doggy…"

And yet one glance at the snarling beast was enough to tell him that this particular specimen was anything *but* a 'nice doggy'; on the contrary, it was his worst nightmare come true.

"Grrrrrr!" replied Max.

Dad took a deep breath. The dog had, he noted to his dismay, taken up a strategic position between his armchair and the door of the shed, thereby blocking his only escape route. *Just try to stay calm* he told himself. *Don't make any sudden movements and everything will be ok.* With beads of cold sweat trickling down his brow, he glanced around. *There – in the corner – a stout broomstick. If he could only somehow reach it, he would at least have a means of defending himself.* Slowly, carefully, hardly daring to breathe, he extended his right arm…

"Grrrrrrr!" Max responded to the movement with another low growl, as if to warn his captive against trying any funny business. Though he had rather enjoyed following the trail of Bingo's Beefy Bites, he had not taken kindly to finding himself suddenly locked up in a small garden shed. And not only was he locked up in a small garden shed, but he was locked up in a small garden shed that contained a strange man - a strange man who persisted in calling him *nice doggy*, a name which no self-respecting canine will tolerate.

"N… N… Nice doggy," Dad repeated, adding insult to injury. *This is it* he thought to himself as his hand closed over the broom handle. *It's now or never...* Though not what anyone would describe as an agile man, he now moved with a speed that would stun any ninja, seizing the broomstick in a sudden, fluid motion. "Ha!" he shouted, triumphantly waggling his new-found weapon in the bulldog's face. "Not so fierce now are you?"

Max studied him quizzically. Whilst he didn't understand quite *why* the strange man was waving a broom at him, he sensed that he was not doing so in the spirit of friendship, and it was with this in mind that he took a menacing step forward and let out a thunderous bark that echoed around the four walls of the shed.

For Dad, whose feeble courage was already at breaking point, this proved to be the final straw. What little fighting spirit he had ever possessed vanished in that instant, the broom falling from his trembling hands with a loud clatter onto the wooden floor. He no longer cared about putting on a show of bravery. He no longer cared if anyone thought him a coward. All he cared about was getting as far away as he possibly could from this terrifying brute.

"Pleeeeeeeese!" he wailed at the top of his voice. "Pleeeeeeese help me!"

Unfortunately for Dad, the one thing that Max hated *even* more than being referred to as a *nice doggy*, was being shouted at for no apparent reason. He had, he felt, put up with this strange man's nonsense for quite long enough, and it was with this in the foremost of his thoughts that he took a menacing step forward and let out a bark that was at least twice as terrifying as his previous effort.

WOOOOOOOF! it boomed.

"Pleeeese!" Dad bawled as he tried in vain to claw his way out through the back wall. *"Someone... Anyone... Heeeeeeelp me!"*

*

Still clutching his precious bone tightly between clenched teeth, Ernie scuttled through the gap in the fence back into his own garden. Hardly daring to breathe, he glanced around. *Where was Max? Could he be lying in wait behind a bush, ready to ambush him?*

"Why, hello there!"

A shrill voice directly behind him sent him leaping skywards like a startled gazelle. Spinning round, Ernie was relieved to see the diminutive figure of Montgomery, perched as ever in his favourite spot on the upturned wheelbarrow.

"Hey," he scolded, dropping the bone at his feet. "What's with all the yelling? You nearly scared me to death!"

"Well that *is* charming," the mouse retorted warmly. "I see you've got your bone back, courtesy of my brilliant scheme, and that's all the thanks I get!"

"I'm sorry," Ernie sighed. "You just scared me, that's all. Thank you."

"You are *most* welcome," Montgomery grinned. "I am only glad to have been of service." He paused, noticing a distinct look of worry on the little dog's face.

"What's the matter?" he squeaked. "You've got your bone back, haven't you?"

"Yes," Ernie replied "but what about Max?"

"What about him?"

"Where is he?" the little dog glanced around nervously. "Didn't you lure him into this garden with those Beefy Bites?"

"Yes, yes, yes," Montgomery chuckled "but you needn't worry about him for the time being. Let's just say he's… He's been *detained*."

"Detained?" Ernie was increasingly baffled. "What do you mean, *detained*?"

"Never mind that," said the mouse. "All you need to know for now is that we needn't worry about Max for the time being. Ok?"

"I suppose so," Ernie agreed, though he sounded far from convinced.

"Good," Montgomery grinned, his voice suddenly taking on a business-like tone "and since my work here is done, perhaps now would be a suitable time to discuss payment for my services."

Ernie frowned.

"Payment?" he shook his head. "I don't understand - you never said anything about wanting money."

"No, no, no," the mouse chuckled. "Of *course* I don't want *money*. What good is money to a mouse of my age, or indeed of *any* age?"

Ernie was growing more confused by the minute.

"Then what *do* you want?" he implored.

"Well, since you ask," answered the mouse "what I would like is this…"

But I am afraid, reader, we will have to wait to find out what it was that Montgomery wanted, for at that precise moment, the conversation was rudely interrupted by a loud commotion from the vicinity of the garden shed.

Ernie pricked up his ears and listened intently. It was a curious, high-pitched squealing kind of noise, the sort of thing one might expect to hear from a startled pig.

"What the dickens was that?" Montgomery frowned. "How very odd. It sounded a bit like a damsel in distress – I never knew we had them in this part the world."

"No," Ernie replied thoughtfully. "I don't think it was that…" The sound was strangely familiar, reminding him of something he had heard only recently. *But what could it be?* Then it came to him; *the last time he had heard a squeal like that had been the other morning when Dad had put his foot in that slipper...*

"Then what was it then?" the mouse persisted. "It certainly sounded like a damsel in distress to me."

"No," the little dog replied, more firmly this time. "It wasn't a damsel in distress – it was Dad! Come on – *quick*, let's go and see what's wrong!"

*

By the time Ernie and Montgomery arrived at the shed, the din coming from the inside had reached a crescendo. The louder Dad yelled, the louder Max barked, and the louder Max barked, the louder Dad yelled, until the very walls of the small wooden building shook as though it had been hit by an earthquake.

"Hmm," Montgomery frowned, scratching his whiskery chin. "It seems as though I might have made a *slight* tactical error."

"What?" Ernie gasped. "Y… You mean you used the trail of Beefy Bites to lead Max into the shed?"

"Yes," the mouse cringed. "That was my plan…"

"And then you bolted the door…"

"Absolutely – it seemed like an excellent means of keeping him out of the way whilst our operation was in progress."

"But Dad was asleep in there!" Ernie shook his scruffy head in dismay. "You've really gone and messed things up now, haven't you?"

"Now just you look here," Montgomery retorted hotly. "How was I supposed to know he was sleeping in there? It's supposed to be a shed, not some sort of hotel! And besides…"

He was interrupted by another ear-splitting shriek from within the confines of the shed.

"Heeeeeeeeeeeelp!" it went.

“Look,” Ernie yapped “we don’t have time to argue. We’ve got to get him out, and quickly by the sounds of it!”

“Very well,” cried the mouse. “Leave it to me!”

Ernie watched in amazement as his friend scurried like a spider, straight up the vertical wall of the shed, gripping the gaps between the planks of wood with his tiny paws. Arriving at the halfway mark, Montgomery halted, pausing only briefly to catch his breath before shimmying over to the large metal bolt that held the door firmly shut.

“You’ll never get that open,” Ernie hissed. “It’s almost as big as you are!”

“Yes,” came the reply. “I must admit it’s a little on the stiff side.”

As the mouse heaved and wrestled with the bolt for all he was worth Dad’s cries from inside the shed grew ever more desperate.

“Come on!” Ernie urged, hopping up and down on his hind legs.

“Grrrr!” Montgomery grunted as he threw every last ounce of strength into his efforts.

We have, reader, already talked about *divine intervention*. Perhaps it now came to the mouse’s aid, or perhaps he was just a great deal stronger than he looked, but either way, just when it seemed like all was lost, there was a groan and a grinding noise, and bolt shot aside with an almighty *thunk.*

"Help!" Montgomery cried as he was catapulted unceremoniously into the nearby compost heap, where he landed with an earthy *PLOP!*

Ernie, however, had more pressing matters on his mind; wide eyed with terror, he watched, rooted to the spot as, with a creak that sent shivers down his spine, the shed door slowly swung open…

Chapter 9

The scene confronting Ernie as he peered into the shed was the sort of thing a television news reporter might describe as a 'tense standoff.' In one corner, having retrieved his broomstick, Dad was brandishing it in the same way that a Zulu warrior might brandish a spear. Max, meanwhile, with his back to the door and oblivious to Ernie's presence, appeared to be stuck in something of a dilemma; his enemy, like Davy Crockett at the Alamo, was cornered with no means of escape, yet there was something about the menacing way in which Dad was waving that broom that gave him pause for thought.

Unsure what to do, Ernie was wondering whether to run to fetch Martha when Dad spotted him through the open door.

"Ernie," he gibbered in a strangled sort of voice. "Ernie please – you've got to help me!"

The little dog looked at him with mixed feelings. Though he sympathised with the man's plight, he could not help but remember some of the hurtful things that

Dad had said in the aftermath of the slipper incident. He had, Ernie recalled, employed a series of fruity words and phrases, many of which he had never heard before, and none of which are suitable to be reproduced in this, a book intended for the younger reader.

"Please!" Dad repeated. "L… Look Ernie – I'm sorry about that business with the slipper. It was my fault – it was stupid of me to leave them lying there on the living room floor like that."

Ernie responded with a haughty *ruff* of agreement. *He knew that Dad would see sense sooner or later…*

"S… So how about we forget all about it, eh?" the stricken man continued. "Let bygones be bygones and all that? Perhaps we could…"

WOOOOOOF!

His voice was drowned out by another thunderous bark from Max.

For Dad, this was simply too much. "Pleeeeeese," he wailed. "Ernie - you can come into the house *every single night!* You can use my slippers as a toilet if you like! You can do *anything* you want, just *please* help me!"

Ernie cocked his ear with interest; this was *much* more like the sort of thing he wanted to hear. Indeed, the generosity of Dad's offer was such that he quickly decided that he would do everything in his power to help. The only question was what, exactly, could a little dog of his small stature do, faced with a monster like Max? As he saw it, the one thing which stood in his favour was the element of surprise; *if he could only sneak up on the huge dog undetected, Ernie felt confident he could give him a shock that he would not forget for a long, long time.* And so, hardly daring to breathe, he crept forward until his little black nose was barely an inch from Max's rear end.

*

Martha surveyed Dad's vegetable patch with a sense of deep satisfaction. *Yes, he might have said something about her not playing with the hose or watering his lettuces, but he couldn't really have meant it. Anyway - that had been almost an hour ago, and it was such a hot, sunny day that it surely wouldn't hurt just to give them a teensy weensy drop. Besides, she was very,*

very, VERY bored, and he was always telling her to make herself useful... And so, unable to resist the allure of the brand new high-powered hose, Martha had diligently set to work. To begin with, she had indeed, watered his precious lettuces sparingly, however this water had quickly drained away into the soil, leaving her (as she saw it) with little option but to add a *teensy weensy* bit more. This pattern of events had continued until, by the time she finally replaced the hose in its holder, Dad's vegetable patch bore a striking resemblance to Lake Windermere. Or Lake Michigan, if you happen to be reading this in the United States.

"Mmm," she pondered to herself. "I wonder if his tomatoes in the greenhouse are ok. I 'spect they could do with a drop of water too." And so off she went down the garden path, dragging the hose behind her.

*

If Max's previous barks had been notable for their loudness, they were mere whispers compared to the ear-splitting howl of agony that he emitted when Ernie's razor sharp teeth clamped firmly down onto his right buttock. With a *YOOOOOWL!* that could be heard in several adjoining counties, he blundered out of the shed, bucking and rearing like an Arab stallion in a frantic bid to dislodge his tormentor. Ernie, however, was equally determined *not* to be dislodged. As he saw it, the longer he could remain attached to the monster's hind quarters, the longer he would be safe from those terrible fangs, and it was with this foremost in his thoughts that he responded to the bucking and rearing by biting down ever harder.

YOOOOOOWL! Max roared again as he began to spin like a top, trying ever more desperately to shake off his attacker. Still, Ernie hung on for dear life, yet he did so with a sinking heart; as the spinning grew ever faster, so he felt the grip of his jaws weakening until, with a final *yip* of dismay, he found himself sailing through the air, finally coming to rest with a juicy *SPLAT* in the compost heap.

"Oof!" came a squeaky voice from somewhere underneath him. "Watch what you're doing!" The voice, of course, belonged to Montgomery; having landed in the compost heap but a few minutes earlier, the unfortunate mouse had only just, with great difficulty, managed to dig his way out of the mud, when he found himself being driven like a tack beneath the stinking surface once again.

But Ernie had no time for apologies. Dusting himself off, he saw to his horror that Max was already bearing down on him, snarling with rage. Pausing only to let out a brief *yip* of alarm, he shot off up the garden path as fast as his little legs would carry him, with the bulldog in hot pursuit. The sound of thundering feet and heavy breathing behind him told him that his enemy was quickly gaining ground; *if only he could make it to the house, perhaps Mum would be able to save him. She was always much braver than Dad in situations like this...*

*

Having arrived at the greenhouse, Martha was reaching for the door handle when she became aware of a strange commotion down at the bottom of the garden. Frowning, she cocked her head and listened. It was a frantic yapping sort of a sound, the kind of noise that a small dog in peril might make, interspersed at regular intervals with the deep booming bark of a much larger specimen. One thing was for sure - whatever it was that was making the commotion was heading her way…

"Ernie!" Martha gasped, her eyes widening as, rounding the bend like a greyhound on a racetrack, the little dog hove into view, his little stumpy legs hammering away for all they were worth. Breathing down his neck, teeth bared, eyes ablaze with fury, there came another, much larger dog, one she had never seen before. Whereas Martha's eyes had initially widened, they now narrowed as her freckled face fixed itself into a look of grim resolve. *So – this horrid brute thinks he's going to hurt Ernie, does he? She would soon see about that…*

*

As he rounded the bend, with the bulldog snapping at his heels, Ernie's life flashed before him. Though he had run as he had never run before, his stumpy little legs had simply not been up to the task. He was a spent force, and any second now, he knew, he would feel the crunch of those terrible jaws upon his person. *Only a miracle could save him now...*

Closing on his prey, Max let out a snarl of triumph. Like most bullies, he was, in his heart of hearts, a coward. Had Ernie been even half his size, the bite on the bottom would have been enough to send him fleeing back to his own garden with little more than a whimper; as it was, he was relishing the prospect of teaching this annoying little pipsqueak a thing or two. It came as a nasty surprise to Max, therefore, when, at the very moment when his victim was almost within his grasp, he was blasted in the face at point-blank range by a raging jet of ice-cold water. The shock as it surged straight up his nostrils and into his mouth was enough to stop him dead in his tracks, just as surely as if he had run into a brick wall.

"Go on!" a voice bellowed through the watery haze. "Get out of here, unless you want some more!"

Choking and spluttering, not knowing what on earth had hit him, Max staggered back a few steps. If there was one thing he *did* know at that particular moment, it was that he did *not* want another blast of that ice-cold water. And so it was with a feeble whimper of surrender that he turned on his tail and fled off down the garden path as fast as his soggy legs would carry him.

"There's a good boy," Martha grinned, flinging the hose to one side and scooping a very grateful Ernie up into her arms. "Did that horrible dog frighten you? Well – I don't think he'll be coming round here again!"

For a few seconds, Ernie snuggled against the little girl, relieved to be back in the safety of her arms. Then a disturbing thought occurred to him; *his bone! He had dropped it somewhere down near the shed moments before he had bitten Max on the bottom. Max had just fled in that very direction. What if he saw it lying on the ground and picked it up? Everything he and Montgomery had worked for would have been in vain!*

With a yip of dismay, he wriggled free of Martha's grip and sped off down the garden path like a whippet.

"Hey!" she yelled. "Ernie – wait!"

But her cries fell on deaf ears. All that Ernie could think about was his beloved bone and he would not rest until it was safely back in his possession…

Chapter 10

Down in the shed, Dad continued to cower. *Sure, Ernie had distracted the big dog, but for how long?* However hard he tried, he couldn't imagine Martha's pet putting up enough of a fight to detain the brute for more than a few seconds, and then what? *Knowing his luck, it would be back, roosting in the shed with him before he knew it - that was what...* And so, with this fear foremost in his thoughts, he had set about feverishly barricading the shed door from the inside with everything he could lay his hands on. Lawnmowers, stepladders, pots of paint – all were used to form a formidable defensive barrier to keep the monster at bay until the Royal Marines (or, for that matter, Mum) came to his rescue. *But wait? What was this? There was something outside – something rattling the door, trying to get in...*

"Nooooo," he shrieked "you'll never take me alive!

The rattling stopped.

"Dad?" Martha sounded puzzled. "Is that you?"

Cautiously, hardly daring to believe his ears, Dad approached the shed door.

"M… Martha?" he called in what can only be described as a broken sob. "Is that you?"

"Yes," a voice boomed through the woodwork. "'Course it is. What are you doing in there? I can't open the door."

"Is… Is it gone?" came the husky reply.

Martha frowned.

"Is what gone?" she said, growing impatient.

"The big dog. Is the big dog gone?"

Martha's frown turned into a grin. Suddenly everything had become clear. *If she played her cards right, she would easily be able to turn this situation to her advantage...*

"Oh yes," she replied "it's gone. You needn't worry – Ernie chased it away."

There followed a great deal of clattering and cursing, accompanied by the sound of heavy objects being dragged aside as the barricade was dismantled. Seconds later, the door creaked open and Dad's head appeared. Wild-eyed and white as a sheet, he reminded Martha of a zombie she had seen in a recent episode of *Scooby Doo*. Grinning from ear to ear, she stood back and watched with mild amusement as he tottered gingerly out into the open, his eyes darting from right to left all the while, as though scarcely able to believe that the ferocious brute had truly been put to flight. It was only after several minutes of tottering, as the mists of terror gradually began to clear, that Dad became aware that his daughter was talking to him.

"So I 'spect you must be feeling pretty guilty about being so mean to Ernie after everything he's done," she was saying. "I 'spect you'll be keen to show him how grateful you are."

Dad goggled at her in bewilderment before transferring his gaze towards the compost heap where a familiar little dog could be observed gnawing with great relish on a yellow rubber bone. Had he looked more closely, he might have noticed that, between gnaws, it appeared to be engaged in an earnest conversation with a small, rather mangy-looking mouse.

"B… B… But…" he gibbered, turning back to his daughter. "I… I mean… *how* did he chase it away?"

"Never mind that," Martha grinned "he just did. Ernie's only small, but he's a lot tougher than he looks, you know."

"Yes but..."

"How about you start by saying 'sorry'?" the little girl continued forcibly.

"Sorry? But..." He gave Martha a pleading look, only to see her freckled features set in that familiar look of steely determination.

"I... I'm sorry, Ernie," he called over to the compost heap in a strangled sort of voice.

"Good," Martha beamed. "Now – let's all go and have some tea, and we can have a nice chat about when he'll be allowed back in the house..."

*

"Right then," said Martha as she guzzled down her last spoonful of desert. "I'm glad that's all settled. Can I leave the table now? I'm off to check if Ernie's ok."

"Yes," Mum nodded with a smile. "Don't be too long, though, because you've homework to finish before bedtime."

"Homework?" Martha turned to direct a fierce scowl at her mother.

"Yes – Have you forgotten? You were supposed to write a diary about your day."

"Oh *that*?" the little girl shrugged. "That won't take long – nothing much has really happened today."

And with this, she left the room, oblivious to the sound of Dad choking violently on his apple crumble.

*

As expected, she found Ernie in his basket in the porch, chewing on his yellow rubber bone with an air of quiet satisfaction. Kneeling down, she was about to give him a friendly tickle behind his ear when a thought occurred to her; *his new pink bone was nowhere to be seen.* The last time she had seen it, it had been in his basket, yet it now appeared to have vanished into thin air.

"Ernie," she said, her eyes narrowing. "Where's your new pink bone?"

As she stroked his back, Martha felt a strong shudder course through his little body at the very mention of the reviled object.

"Where is it?" she repeated. "I understand if you don't like it, and I don't mind if you've hidden it, but I just want to know where it is."

Ernie, however, was deaf to her pleas. As far as he was concerned, the monstrous *Pretender to the Bone* had been suitably disposed of; it had passed from his life once and for all, and he wanted nothing more to do with it. And so, with a stubborn shrug, he assumed an expression of innocence and resumed his tender gnawing.

The mystery of the vanishing pink bone was not one which would have taxed Sherlock Homes. Indeed, Martha had barely set foot in the garden when its final resting place became blatantly obvious.

"Oh no!" she gasped, clutching her head in her hands. "Oh Ernie – how *could* you?"

For there, right in the middle of the front lawn, were signs that the little dog had been extremely busy whilst they had been having their evening meal. Determined that the ghastly abomination should never again see the light of day, he had dug deep, deeper than he had ever dug in his entire life, and Martha had an uneasy suspicion that Dad would not appreciate the resulting mountain of earth that had become a new, predominant feature of his lawn. She frowned, thinking hard. *If her father saw this, Ernie's standing in the Miller household would be forever ruined. He would, for want of a better expression be 'in the dog house.' Could the mysterious mountain of soil be passed off as a mole hill? Perhaps it could, except Dad would be sure to investigate the hole, and the minute he found that pink bone, Ernie would be banged to rights. Not even she, with all her persuasive powers, could persuade him that a mole had somehow entered their house, taken the pink bone from Ernie's basket and buried it in the middle of the front lawn. No – there was only one thing for it – she would have to act, and act fast...* And so, with a look of grim determination, Martha stomped off down to the shed to fetch a spade.

Just as Ernie had done before her, she dug, and she dug, and she dug some more, always casting nervous glances towards the house, dreading the sound of heavy footsteps approaching down the path. Fortunately for Martha, though she did not know it, there was a football game on the television that night which would keep Dad safely out of the picture for much of the evening. All around her, dusk was setting in, the skies darkening as a nearby blackbird tootled a final tune before turning in for the night. And still there was no sign of the bone… It was only when she was on the verge of giving up, cross, weary and coated from head to toe in mud, that she spotted a glimpse of pink shining up at her through the murk.

"Yes!" she yelled, sending the dozing blackbird fluttering skyward with a cry of alarm. Lying flat on her stomach, heedless to the vast quantities of soil on her face, clothes and in hair, Martha reached down into the void and grasped the bone in her grubby hand.

But what now? How could she dispose of the evidence? There was no point in taking it back to the house – Ernie simply would not tolerate it. Nor could she return it to the shop for a refund – Mr Longbottom had, after all, let her have it for free. Then a thought occurred to her; *that dog next door. It had seemed like a horrid creature, but maybe it was just lonely. Maybe it didn't have a kind owner who loved it as she did Ernie. Maybe it would appreciate a new rubber bone, even if it WAS a pink one...* And so, just as she had done a few short days ago, she drew back her right arm and, with the power and technique of an Olympic shot-putter, launched the bone high over the fence and into next-door's garden.

"There!" she grinned, rubbing her hands with satisfaction. "All sorted – now I s'pose I'd better get that hole filled in before Dad sees..."

Epilogue

Ernie and Martha were not the only ones who had been busy that evening. In a little hole in the ground underneath Dad's shed, Montgomery had also been working tirelessly. When he had earlier mentioned 'payment' for his services, all he had, in fact, wanted was a guarantee from Ernie that he would be allowed to set up home beneath the shed in the Miller's garden without fear of being evicted as he had been from his previous residence round at Old Mrs Wiseman's. Ernie, of course, had been more than happy to grant him his wishes, the little dog having high hopes of a long and happy friendship that would stretch far ahead into the future.

"Ah yes," the mouse sighed with deep satisfaction as he tucked himself into his tiny bed of straw. "This is just the place for me."

There is an old saying from the Scottish poet Robert Burns which suggests that "the best-laid plans of mice and men often go awry," meaning that, however carefully we plan something, there is still a chance that it could all go horribly wrong. As he nodded off to sleep that evening, Montgomery reflected that, whilst this may indeed be true with respect to mice and *men,* the best-laid plans of mice and *dogs* generally seemed to work out rather well…

*

An outsider peering into the living room of the Miller household that evening, would have witnessed what, at a glance, appeared to be a scene of perfect tranquillity and domestic bliss. In an armchair in the corner of the room, a man sat in his dressing gown and slippers, gazing at the television, showing no outward signs of the harrowing ordeal through which he had passed but a few short hours beforehand. Directly opposite him, reclining sleepily in a second armchair, a lady, also clad in a dressing gown, was apparently deeply absorbed in a paperback novel. On the big leather sofa nearest the fireplace, meanwhile, there lay a little girl in a purple nightie. And on her knee, gnawing contentedly on a yellow rubber bone whilst he watched the television, there nestled a small, brown, somewhat scruffy-looking dog. All in all then, as previously stated, a scene of tranquillity and domestic bliss. *Or was it?*

In actual fact, only three out of the four bodies present could be described as truly happy. Martha was happy because Ernie had once more been reinstated in his rightful position on her lap. Mum was happy simply because Martha was happy. And Ernie – what can we say about Ernie other than that he was in a state of unbridled, heavenly bliss. Not only was he back in the warmth of the living room, snug and warm on Martha's lap, but he had also been reunited with the one and only love of his life – his yellow rubber bone. *Could things get any better than this?*

But what of Dad? I hear you ask. Well, reader, as for Dad, he had decidedly mixed feelings about the day's events. Yes – he grudgingly accepted that Ernie had done him a favour by chasing the vicious dog away, however he only had Martha's word on this, and held sneaking suspicions that she may not have *quite* told the truth, the whole truth and nothing but the truth of the matter. In addition to this vague feeling that he had somehow been tricked, he was annoyed that Ernie's original crime of pooping in his slipper appeared to have been completely forgotten by the rest of the family. *What,* he asked himself, *was civilization coming to when such a heinous act could go unpunished?* It was in this dark and brooding frame of mind that, as the ten o'clock news ended, he rose stiffly from his chair and muttered something about heading up to bed for an early night, pausing only to cast a withering glance at the little girl and her dog as he headed out of the door.

*

In his kennel in next door's garden, Max closed his eyes with a sleepy sigh and thought about his day. Sure, it had started promisingly when he had found a yellow rubber bone in his garden. Although it had been dirty, chewed up and clearly past its sell-by date, he had never owned a rubber bone before and had been most delighted with his discovery. Following this, however, things had quickly taken a turn for the worst. The next thing he knew, he had awoken from his mid-morning nap only to find a horrid little dog attempting to steal it from him. Shortly after this, he had been lured from his home by a dastardly trick and locked up in a shed with a strange man who had, for reasons Max failed to understand, insisted on waving a broomstick in his face. As if that wasn't bad enough, he had then been bitten on the bottom by the very same wicked little dog that had earlier tried to steal his bone, the whole ordeal being rounded off with a jet of ice-cold water in the face. By the time he had returned to his kennel, Max had cut a sad, soggy and broken figure. *Why did everything in his life seem to turn out wrong? Why, oh why, couldn't something nice happen to him, just for once?*

But at that very moment, just when he had been wallowing in the deepest depths of despair, something nice *had* happened to him. As if sent from the Gods, a pink rubber bone had come hurtling out of nowhere and landed on the patio right in front of his very nose. Scarcely able to believe his eyes, Max had crept forward and given it a tentative sniff. It had *smelled* real. Then he had licked it. It had *tasted* real. It *was* real – his very own rubber bone! Furthermore, it wasn't a dirty, tatty old chewed-up thing like the one he'd found before – this was brand new! *Oh joy of joys – Lady Luck had found him at last!* As he drifted off to sleep, Max's last thought was that it perhaps wasn't such a bad world after all…

*

The next day dawned bright and fair. After a restless night, tormented by nightmares of fiendish, snarling dogs, Dad was nevertheless the first to awaken in the Miller household. Descending the stairs, he crossed the hall and, as was his usual practice, donned his slippers on his way through to the kitchen. But as he did so, he experienced the distinctly unpleasant sensation of something squelching between his toes…

"*MARTHA!*" he shrieked, tearing the slipper off as he hopped madly around the hallway. "*MARTHA!* Get down here at once! That blasted dog of yours has only gone and done it *again*!"

*

Through in the porch, awoken by the commotion out in the hallway, Ernie sat up in his basket. Cocking his head to one side, he listened with growing interest to Dad's rantings and ravings, which were soon joined by the sound of Martha's voice, rising in protest. Amidst the din, one word in particular kept cropping up; 'slippers'. For some strange reason, Dad seemed deeply unhappy about his slippers. Ernie gave his bone a thoughtful nibble. *What was the matter with the old so-and-so now? Surely he hadn't already forgotten that there were not one, but* ***two*** *parts to the deal they had struck down at the shed the previous afternoon.* The first, that Ernie should be allowed back into the house, Dad had duly honoured; the second, relating to the shared use of the tartan size-tens, he appeared to have forgotten completely! *Human beings,* the little dog concluded, *were a curious species; highly intelligent in many ways, but a little dumb in others.* With a sigh of anticipation, Ernie gave his beloved bone another tender nibble as he readied himself for what promised to be another interesting day with the Millers…

The End

Other titles by James Sutherland

Norbert's Summer Holiday

Christmas with Norbert

Norbert to the Rescue!

Norbert's Spooky Night

Norbert - The Collection

The Further Adventures of Roger the Frog

Frogarty the Witch

The Tale of the Miserous Mip

Jimmy Black and the Curse of Poseidon

About the Author

James Sutherland was born in Stoke-on-Trent, England, many, many, many years ago. So long ago, in fact, that he can't remember a thing about it. The son of a musician, he moved around lots as a youngster, attending schools in the Isle of Man and Spain before returning to Stoke where he lurked until the age of 18. After gaining a French degree at Bangor University, North Wales, James toiled manfully at a variety of office jobs before making a daring escape through a fire exit, hell-bent on writing silly nonsense full-time. In his spare time, James enjoys hunting for slugs in the garden, chatting with his gold fish and frolicking around the house in his tartan nightie.

Visit www.jamessutherlandbooks.com for more information and all the latest news!

Printed in Great Britain
by Amazon